His Death Sentence

His Death Sentence

A Novel written by:

Tabitha Greer

authorHOUSE®

AuthorHouse™
1663 Liberty Drive
Bloomington, IN 47403
www.authorhouse.com
Phone: 1-800-839-8640

First published by AuthorHouse   07/25/2011

ISBN: 978-1-4634-4153-1 (sc)
ISBN: 978-1-4634-4152-4 (hc)
ISBN: 978-1-4634-4151-7 (ebk)

Library of Congress Control Number: 2011913193

Printed in the United States of America

Any people depicted in stock imagery provided by Thinkstock are models, and such images are being used for illustrative purposes only.
Certain stock imagery © Thinkstock.

This book is printed on acid-free paper.

CONTENTS

Chapter One
FIGHTING BEGINS

"What? Abby come on, are you sure Jonny said that about you?" asked Maggie Matthews, curiously through the phone.

"Yes, I'm sure! Look, ask your parents if you can stay sometime this weekend, okay?" pleaded Abby.

Abby sat on her orange polka dotted bed and thought *oh please let Maggie come over! I want her to stay so we can have some fun. It's been a week or two since we've had girl night. Maybe I could even invite some of our other girlfriends to join us. I wonder what Robert will say about Maggie coming over. I know he likes her, they've been friends forever. I don't see why they don't go on and start dating.*

"Sure. How about Saturday night? Let me see what I can do because mom and dad haven't been the best of company to be around lately."

"Saturday sounds good. Let me guess; they're still fighting? Hey what's that sound?"

"It's probably mom and dad fighting, again. It's a typical thing for them anymore. They're fighting constantly and I'm getting sick and tired of this. Oh here's Alex. I'd better go. I love you girl."

"Love you too, Maggie," exclaimed Abby worriedly. Abby tossed her cell to the edge of her bed, slid the remote off her night stand, and turned the channel to CMT.

Maggie glanced at her diary and pushed it away with her feet not feeling the urge to write at the moment. She hung up her phone as Alex jumped on her bed. She whispered staring into her little brother's beautiful sea-green eyes.

"What's wrong?" Maggie asked as she tousled Alex's dirty blonde curls, wishing that her hair was like her brother's.

"Mom and dad are fighting again. Why do they fight?" questioned Alex nervously. He sat there cradled in his sister's arms, silently crying. Maggie ran her fingers through his soft, blonde curls. She tousled it about and thought, *why do my parents even fight? What's the point in it? Something has to be done about all of this.* She gave Alex a smile so he wouldn't feel discouraged, "Sometimes parents have differences, even though they might love each other, they will fight no matter what. Sometimes those differences can get in the way of their marriage or they could simply have a disagreement about something. Do you understand?"

"Sort of, I guess," murmured Alex.

Maggie whispered softly. "Where's Joe? He usually comes in here too." *Where is your big brother at? He knows the rules but yet he continues to disregard them.*

"Didn't he come and tell you?"

"Tell me what?" asked Maggie hurriedly. She brushed back some hair behind her ears concern transforming her face. She stared Alex straight in the eyes.

"That he was planning to sneak out his window over to Robert's house for a few hours until our parents have calmed down. At least that's what he said."

"Oh! Oh, okay because I was just wondering. You say he went exactly where?" Alex ignored her question.

"It sounds like they've stopped. I'm going to go see, Maggie. You stay here sissy. Okay?"

"Alex be careful, please? If they start fighting or yelling again, go to your room."

"Okay," exclaimed Alex. He jumped off her bed his feet landing loudly on the hardwood floor and dashed out of her room. Alex returned, knocked on the door, and popped his little head in. He whispered, "They've stopped. They're sitting down talking to one another." Maggie nodded her head in approval just as Alex softly shut her door. Maggie slipped out of her room down the hall and stood waiting impatiently in front of Joe's door. She knocked,

"Who is it and what do you want?" Joe called aggressively.

"Hey, open up; it's me, Maggie. Come on Joe, I know you're in there! I heard the window shutting."

"Coming, hang on," hollered her big brother. He flung his door open and Maggie slipped inside, getting straight to the point.

"You went over to Robert's, didn't you? Did anybody else see you, besides Alex?"

"No. I was very careful *baby* sis," answered Joe with a sigh.

"That's good to know. Why won't they just go to a marriage counselor like we told them?" quizzed Maggie. She glanced about his room taking in the scenery and was appalled. *Why does he have to do these things?* The items that she took most notice of were a couple of empty glass bottles ranging from tequila to vodka and a couple of empty packs of Marlboro red cigarettes. She took a few steps toward Joe and stepped on something squishy and she closed her eyes. *I don't even want to look down.* She sucked in a deep breath and opened her eyes glancing downward. What she saw was something that she prayed that she wouldn't ever see again; a used condom.

"Because they're stupid, need another reason, Maggie?" She looked up into Joe's eyes and asked, "What the hell is this Joe?"

"What the hell is what?"

Maggie pointed to the appalling object and Joe replied, "Oh that. Um . . . do you want the truth?"

"No . . . just forget that I ever asked anything about it."

"Okay. Anyways like I was saying, Robert told me to tell you to call him. I'm going to take a shower if you don't mind." He grabbed a pair of checkered boxers and white t-shirt and stepped out of his room across the hall to the bathroom.

Maggie walked out his room. Before she left she took one final look at Joe's room and shook her head in disapproval. She returned to her more appealing and comfortable room. Her cell phone began ringing. She ran to her dresser, almost knocking her picture frames off the shelf. She grabbed her cell. "Hello?"

"Hey Maggie what are you? I heard your parents were having another fight. Is everything alright? How's Alex, my little buddy doing?"

"Hey Robert, I'm fine. Why did you call me?" Maggie questioned curiously her hopes rising.

"I just called to talk," murmured Robert with a grin. He sat in his chair in front of his computer starring at a picture of Maggie in a purple polka dotted bikini. He smiled at the picture, knowing the only reason why she wore the bikini in the first place because he bought it for her birthday last summer.

"Okay well I'm just scared only when Dad gets mad. You know he used to be in the military and he also used to be a boot camp officer or something like that. He has a really loose and horrible temper so he just scares me. Joe and I've talked to them and tried persuading them to go to a marriage counselor together, but as stubborn as they are, they won't go. Alex; it scares him and he cries almost every time they fight," whispered Maggie sadly. "I don't think they know how bad it scares and hurts him."

"Maggie you know that you are allowed over whenever they start fighting to just hang out. Even Alex," exclaimed Robert in amusement. He thought *I would love it if you came over here. We could have some fun.* He smiled to himself.

"What would your parents think?" muttered Maggie curiously.

"They wouldn't care. Abby told them about your parents always at each other's throat." Maggie made a sound in protest. "Well Maggie it seems like it, doesn't it? Anyway, next time this happens, sneak out your window with Alex and Joe, okay," urged Robert.

"Sure I guess so. Hey, what are you doing tomorrow night?" asked Maggie. She giggled and rolled her eyes up towards the ceiling and wondered *I hope he says nothing. Oh I pray that he does.* She sat there hugging her stuffed, plush frog to her chest and just smiled to herself.

"I'm going to the movies with Joe, Abby, my parents, and you of course. I couldn't forget you," whispered Robert slyly.

"I know; well I have to be going, alright? See you tomorrow."

"See you, goodnight." whispered Robert. He sat there thinking, *I wonder why she asked me that for. I know she likes me, but she told Abby, she didn't like me enough to go out with me. Hmmm . . .* wondered Robert as he sat down at his desk. He stomped his cigarette out in the ashtray and smiled to himself in satisfaction.

He logged onto his Facebook web page and as he was shifting through and reading his e-mails, he didn't hear Abby slip into his room. She snuck up behind him, yelling, "Ah!" He jumped out of his seat screaming.

"What the shit Abby? Are you crazy? You can't just sneak up on somebody. Got it?" He plopped back down into his seat, and Abby looked over her brother's shoulder curiously to read his e-mails. The one on the screen made Abby whisper.

"Oh . . . I'm telling mom. You've been drinking beer again."

"No I haven't."

"Yes you have. It even says so right here in this paragraph. See?" She pointed to it and Robert immediately deleted that message. He spun around in his seat, leaped at his sister and grabbed her by the throat muttering angrily, "If you ever tell mom, I'm going to tell her about that boy you've been talking to and sneaking around with down at the drag strip. You know he's only seventeen. See if she likes that, huh? Oh and what's this I've been hearing about you sneaking out with Joe at midnight? What do you have to say about that?"

"Nothing, that's absurd and who did you even hear that from?"

"Joe."

"Whatever . . ." replied Abby sarcastically. "Robert, I don't go around asking you what you do with your spare time, do I? No, I didn't think so."

"No. Fine, shake, and spit. Call truce." So Robert and Abby spit on each other's hands and then shook. With that Abby walked out. She turned and glared at him evilly; walking down the hall, she thought, *that's blackmail. I still think mom should know about him drinking, but I don't want her or dad for that matter to know about Johnny. He's really a great guy, yeah he might be kind of old for me but still, I don't care. Anyways, I hope Maggie's parents said yes.*

Chapter Two
UNDERCOVER PARTY

"Mom . . . Dad can I stay at Abby's house tonight? Her parents said that I could. So can I? Please? Joe wants to stay the night with Robert. Is that okay too?" pleaded Maggie. Her parents looked at one another.

Her mother, Claire replied, "Um, honey we have something to tell you." Maggie sat down at the kitchen table and glanced from her mom to her dad. "Your father and I have decided to go to marriage counseling like you and Joe asked us to do months ago. We have an appointment at noon today. So, yes I guess it wouldn't hurt, would it Dave?"

"I don't see why not," answered her father as he stood up to put on his jacket.

"Also their parents want to take us to the movies with them. Is that alright?" pleaded Maggie.

Her parents looked at one another again and Clare replied, "Sure. We have to be going now but we're taking Alex to stay at your grandmother's house tonight. You and Joe can watch the house or go over to the ball park in town. Okay? Just be careful about riding your four-wheelers over to the park. I don't want to get another phone call about you two from the police. Got it?" warned their mom as she walked into the living room.

"What did I do?" asked Joe descending down the staircase.

"Nothing, I hope," declared Dave, their father grimacing as he spoke to his son.

"Yes, mom, we completely understand you; you can trust us," declared Maggie confidently as she gave her mom a hug and a peck on the cheek.

"Well I wouldn't go so far to say that but I'll accept your word," replied Clare. She hugged her daughter back and gave her a light peck on the cheek before she walked out the front door into the brilliant, sunlight. Her father followed suit but not before giving Maggie a quick hug and kiss on the forehead. He closed the door behind him as he walked out.

"Where are they going?" asked Joe as he planted his behind on the couch.

"To a marriage counselor; they talked about it and finally agreed." Maggie shrugged her shoulders as she sat down beside Joe.

"Well it's about damn time," muttered Joe impatiently.

"You're telling me? Anyway, mom told me that we are allowed to ride our four-wheelers over to the ballpark, but to be careful or just stay here."

"Really . . . I'm calling Robert and a couple of the other guys over.

"Um . . . hello? What about me?" asked Maggie, jumping up and waving her hands in front of her brother's face.

"What about you?"

"Would it be alright if I invited some of my girls over?"

"I don't care what the hell you do as long as you stay out of my way and don't get the cops called on us or you."

"Whatever," replied Maggie; she ran up the stairs to her room to make a few phone calls.

Hey Robert do you want to come over?" asked Joe.

"Sure . . . is Maggie going to be there?"

"Of course; hey be here in about an hour."

"Cool. See you then." Robert got off the phone, looked at that picture of Maggie again and just smiled gleefully to himself.

Maggie you look hot! I love your outfit!" declared Lisa excitedly over the blaring radio. "Whose idea was it to throw a party?"

"Thanks! It was Joe's idea, who else?"

"You even got your parents out of the house for a few hours," shouted Beth into Maggie's ear.

"That was my idea. I admit it took longer than I planned but hey, I'm not complaining! Anyway, are you having fun?"

"Yeah, it's a blast. Thanks for inviting us!" yelled Lisa.

"Hey Maggie, come here!" yelled Joe.

"Hang on, okay? I'll be right back in a few," muttered Maggie not in the slightest amused.

Maggie walked away and passed a few of her other friends, waving at them as she went. *Somebody has dimmed the lights again* thought Maggie. She walked in the guys' direction where a couch, was propped against a wall in the basement. Joe, Dally, and of course Robert all beamed up at her as she stood in front center of them throwing her hands to her hips starring down at them angrily. Robert thought *Man does she look hot. I love that dress on her body. It does wonderful things to her figure. The length, it's so short. I think it might be one of those mini dresses . . . maybe.* His eyes roamed over her body hungrily, taking in every curve of her body, every little detail he devoured from her; unknowingly she was returning the same treatment.

He noticed the way that the dress hugged the top of her hips and showed off her firm, tight small waist, but flowing out around her thighs. *Its cut so low, maybe I should drop something down the front?* Hearing Joe's voice brought him out of his world and back into reality.

"Do you know Dally?" Joe asked Maggie.

"Um . . . yeah duh, I met him last summer, remember? He said that I was hot and didn't believe you that I was your sister," explained Maggie in frustration. *Men! Why do they exist? Oh yeah . . . so they can act like they rule the earth and everything in their path, along with seducing us for their own pleasures.*

"Well oh yeah. Anyways, Robert has a question for you. Go on and ask her."

"No I don't. Dude, what, are you talking about?" questioned Robert.

Joe looked at him dumbfounded and winked at him twice Robert finally understood what he was getting at, and piped up, saying, "I'll just ask her later. Not here in front of everybody. I don't want to embarrass her."

"Um . . . hello? I'm standing right here. Could you at least look at me and just say what you want to say?"

"Fine if you won't man, I will because she's a hot chick and I'm not going to let her walk away from my hands like you."

"Like hell you aren't!" declared Robert.

Maggie stood there shooting daggers at each and every one of them. She said, "Fine, you guys have just wasted my time. Do you know that? No, of course not, because you're all just sitting there arguing back and forth about who's going to ask me a stupid question. Well guess what, neither one of you are going to have the privilege to ask me." With that being the final word, she turned on her heel, and stalked away.

Robert stood up, trailing after her, and grabbed her arm once he reached her. "Meet me at the old bar tonight." whispered Robert hotly in her ear. She felt his arm slide around her waist and felt his fingers curl themselves around her slender, bony hip. "Make sure nobody sees you okay?"

"Okay," whispered Maggie softly. She looked up at him and thought, *why does he want me to meet him at the old bar tonight? If he tries any funny business I'm leaving.* He let her go and headed toward the downstairs kitchen where Maggie could see the guys getting something out of the cabinets and pouring it into their red plastic, Dixie cups. *Probably alcohol . . .*

Robert looked her way, searching her face for some kind of emotion other than madness. It wasn't working so he gave up. She turned around and left him starring at her backside. As Maggie turned, her dress swirled around her allowing Robert to become entranced with her long legs and the sway of her hips and her firm, round bottom pushing the dress up and making it appear shorter than it originally was designed to be. He couldn't look away.

As the guys were making their way back to the couch to sit back down, Robert declared abruptly, "Joe, man I'm sorry to say this but your sister is hot. She is fine as wine."

"So you keep telling me and not doing anything with her or to her. I need to get her off my case. She follows me around like a little puppy looking for its parents."

"I'll be her . . ." exclaimed Dally.

"Please, don't say what I think you were going to say," warned Joe.

"I'm taking her to the old bar tonight. I asked her to meet me there." said Robert.

Maggie watched the guys talking. She wondered what they were smirking about and why they kept throwing glances her way. Out of nowhere Hope, Krissy and Abby showed up.

"Where is Robert?" questioned Maggie curiously.

"I don't know." Somebody came up behind her, wrapped an arm around her waist, pulled her to his body, and whispered huskily in her ear, "Care to dance?"

"With you? Drop dead!" She turned her head slightly and Robert grabbed her by the chin and turned her face so she was starring him dead set in the eye. He said forcefully, "You're going to dance with me; got it and not another word about it." She thought *okay maybe I do need to dance with him.*

"Come on let's go." Joe was standing by watching Robert lead Maggie out onto the middle of the basement floor. He saw Robert pull Maggie into a tight embrace and turned his attention to Dally bumping him in the ribs in doing so. Dally turned around and looked at Maggie and Robert and whispered harshly, "Man, he's ruined my chances of dating your sister."

"What made you think that you had any chance with my sister pal? You thought all wrong, man." declared Joe protectively.

"Oh okay, I see how . . ." his words were cut off by Dally shouting, "Hey Joe, when were your parents suppose to be home?"

"They said not for a few hours. Why?"

"Well because they've just pulled into the driveway."

"Shit! Hey everybody upstairs, right now, quick!" Joe rushed everybody upstairs and then he hollered, "Just sit down and act cool and calm; like nothing ever happened." Dally and Joe raced back downstairs, Dally missed a few steps along the way. He tripped and fell tumbling down the stairs. Joe ended up falling down the stairs right behind Dally and landed squarely on top of him. Dally murmured, "Get your skinny, bony ass off me!"

"Oh alright," exclaimed Joe rudely. He bolted up, running for the stereo, turned it off, and ran back upstairs. Dally ran a few steps behind Joe, appeared and asked rather shakily, "What do you want me to do with all this alcohol?"

"Um, hide it upstairs in my room under my bed." Dally was gone in a flash up to Joe's bedroom.

"They're here at the door!" yelled Big D. He leaned against the wall for support, acting all innocent.

"Hello. Anybody home?" rang Clare's voice.

"Hey mom, we got bored so we invited some friends over so we could all enjoy some movies together," answered Joe with a nervous smile.

"Okay. I know that I might be regretting to ask this question but it needs to be asked. Did you all behave?"

"Yes, Mrs. Matthews. Dally, Max, Johnny, and I were the supervisors seeing as how we're the oldest. We just decided it should be us," declared Big D raising his hand and saying, "I'm Big D." Max and the other boys followed Big D's example by identifying themselves.

"Well, I guess we'd better be going, shouldn't we?" suggested Dally.

"Yes, I think that is a great idea," said Mrs. Matthews nervously.

Joe and Maggie walked their friends to the door and said bye, but Robert stayed behind way longer than anybody else. He stepped toward Maggie and said, "Come here." She filled in those last few inches between them and Robert drew her into his arms and gave her a slight hug.

Maggie murmured, "You'd better be going before my dad thinks we're up to something. Okay?"

"I'll leave if you really want me to. Alright; just one more thing though." He ran his fingers through her soft, curly blonde hair.

"Oh, and what would that happen to be?"

"This." Robert leaned down and kissed Maggie gently on the lips. He thought to himself, *she tastes so delicious or is it just her watermelon lip gloss that she's wearing? Naw, it's her naturally.* Maggie backed up quickly and declared astonished, "What the hell was that for, Robert?"

"What? It was just a friendly kiss."

"I highly doubt that. That was no friendly kiss. Do you want to know what a friendly kiss qualifies as?" Robert opened his mouth to speak but Maggie cut him off and said, "A friendly kiss is when someone just kisses you on the cheek or the forehead."

Is he really that stupid; he's making me so mad right now, but wait why am I getting all upset over a kiss for? Oh that's right, because he kissed me on the lips. What the freaking hell is wrong with him? I bet him anything that my dad is standing there watching us right now.

"Well hey babe, I ought to be going. My parents are texting me saying it's time to come home to get ready for tonight."

"Okay," muttered Maggie shooting flames at his backside as he bounded down their front porch steps. Joe sat beside her on the porch swing, staring at the sunset.

She thought helplessly, *why can't I find a decent guy who doesn't or won't take advantage of me? Find a guy who will sit here on the swing with me like*

Joe and watch the sun set with me. Now Joe isn't the type of guy that I would like to date either. He's not as bad as Robert, but close enough.

Joe turned and looked at the right side of her face and thought *he saw a tear or two drop from her eyes.* He spoke up and said, "So what are you and Robert going to do tonight?"

Maggie looked at him straight in the eye and declared, "Joe, tell me something. Why do you smoke and drink and everything else that you do that I may not know about?"

"I can't answer that question. I guess in the end what it all really comes down to is that it makes me feel cool, look cool, and on top of that it makes me have this feeling like I have power, endless power," Joe replied knowingly.

Maggie stood up and declared, "That is the most ridiculous idea I have heard from you so far."

He just remained sitting and laughing at her. She thought *what's so funny?* Joe said, "If you did the things that I do, you'd understand what I mean."

"Yeah but I'm not that stupid to smoke or anything else for that matter." With that being said, Maggie stepped inside the house and eased herself into the lounge chair.

"Hey, move your head. I can't see the screen mister!" yelled Mr. Anderson.

"I'm sorry," answered the man sarcastically. He stood up, got out of his seat, and trailed down the aisle to the lobby.

"I like this movie; it's funny," whispered Abby to Maggie without taking her eyes off the screen.

"Yeah, tell me about it." She glanced at Robert and noticed that he was asleep. Abby felt Maggie jab her in the ribs and looked over and whispered,

"What was that for?"

"Oh nothing; it's just that I wanted to let you know that your brother is asleep with his head on Joe's shoulder; He's drooling and his hand is covering Joe's."

Abby glanced at Robert and Joe, wondering if her mental image that Maggie explained was the same. *Pretty much,* thought Abby, and then she burst out laughing.

"Hey, why are you laughing? What's so funny?" asked Mrs. Anderson curiously.

"It's Robert. Look!" Mr. Anderson declared, "The movie is over ya'll. Come on let's go home kids."

"Alright but first wake the boys up." Mrs. Anderson stood to leave and the girls followed her example. She started to the aisle but stayed where she stood once Mr. Anderson said, "Why, me?"

"Because I said so, do you need another reason why?" When she didn't receive an answer from her husband, she walked away knowing that the matter was settled. Maggie and Abby followed Mrs. Anderson to the Black, Yukon XL.

They crawled inside the vehicle and sat there patiently waiting for the boys to come out. Mr. Anderson, Robert, and Joe jumped inside. The boys sat looking from their mom to Abby to Maggie and wondering why they were smiling such big wide grins. Abby handed Joe her digital camera and seeing the picture of them together sleeping, they felt so embarrassed. Robert threw the camera at Abby and commanded, "Delete that picture now!"

"No, make me!" Abby replied, sticking her tongue out at him. Mr. Anderson declared abruptly, "Either you two behave or I'm taking Maggie and Joe home immediately."

That silenced Robert and Abby, but not their devilish, sly looks they kept flashing each other.

Chapter Three
MIDNIGHT MEET

Beep, beep, beep vibrated Maggie's cell. She slipped as quietly as she possibly could from the top bunk to find her Nike, pink over-night bag. She carried it to the bathroom which connected to Abby's room. Once inside, Maggie flipped the light switch on, glancing around nervously in her bag for that one favorite button up, spaghetti strap tank top. It was strawberry red, with her mini, blue jean cut off shorts.

Maggie slid her cell and switchblade into her back left pocket along with one of her I-pods. She carried her socks and cowgirl boots in hand as she descended down the staircase to the kitchen. She crept over to the back door and tried the handle. It was unlocked so Maggie slipped outside quietly. She pulled her socks on and shoved her feet into the boots.

At the end the driveway, she stopped to check if anybody was following her. Nobody was in sight so she continued on her way. Maggie couldn't help but think *the old rundown bar is just right up the road. I'm kinda scared now. It's all dark and I just hope that all Robert wants to do is just talk.*

So she pulled out her I-pod and played Carrie Underwood's song, "Before he Cheats" the lyrics singing lightly through the earphones. As she walked up to the shaggy, dry rotted bar, she noticed a shadow strolling lazily towards her. She stopped the song and shouted, "Hello? Robert is that you?"

"Yes. Come on inside!" shouted Robert calmly. He stood leaning against the frame of the doorway and gazed deeply at Maggie, his eyes raking over her body seductively. Her eyes questioned him. "Aren't you going to join me, I won't bite." His eyes telling a different story than what his lips were proclaiming. Robert turned, his shadow slipping away, leaving Maggie to contemplate what she wanted to do.

Maggie carefully stepped inside, across the threshold and found Robert sitting relaxed in a chair. A six pack of Budweiser sitting beside him.

"You look good Maggie, real good. Come and sit down. Have a beer," urged Robert. He gazed at her longingly and thought *I would love it if we were together. Then I really could have my way with her.*

"Um, no thank you. Why did you ask me to come out here Robert?"

"Just so we can go for a walk together. Is that all right?" questioned Robert. He noticed her outfit and commented. "I love your tank top. Why don't you come a little closer?"

"Oh, yeah sure what do you think I am, stupid?" replied Maggie sarcastically.

"I just want to talk to you," whispered Robert sternly. He gazed at her and wondered *what she's thinking. I would love to know that. That'd be the day.*

"Okay," murmured Maggie to herself. "This sure was a weird place for us to meet." He got up, grabbed a beer, draped an arm around her shoulders and pulled the tab on the beer can. They stepped across the threshold out into the midnight air, stars twinkling down upon them, the full moon lighting their way along the dirt road. Robert pushed the already opened beer can under Maggie's nose, her hand automatically coming up, and pushing it away from her face.

She commented sure of herself, "I said no Robert and I'm not going to tell you again."

His hand twisted within Maggie's hair, jerking her head back ordering, "Don't get lippy with me again . . . do you understand me?"

"Yes!" answered Maggie sharply through clenched teeth.

"Good." Robert released her hair, laying his arm back across her shoulders, pulling Maggie tightly to his side. "Well I'm ready. How about you baby?"

"Ready for what?" whispered Maggie disgustedly. "I knew it was stupid of me to come down here when it's obviously clear you only want one thing from me." Robert stopped walking, stood quietly thinking *she is pushing my buttons, I'm trying to remain calm though.*

Maggie stood there, her body pressed against his side listening intently to his deep, slow breaths and the crickets chirping softly around them in the midnight summer heat. She dared a quick glance at Robert but looked away quickly as her eyes locked on his. Maggie looked down at the road, and felt herself blushing.

Robert pulled his thoughts and anger back together. He replied innocently, "Now why would I want that when I can get any girl I want?"

"I have no idea. Why don't you tell me?" demanded Maggie angrily. "Because as of right now I'm ashamed of myself for sneaking out in the middle of the night to meet up with you."

He caught Maggie by her upper arm, halted her to a stop and turned her to face him. He tossed his beer can to the ground. Maggie noticed the look on his face told her that he was serious.

Robert brought his hand to her cheek whispering, "so soft." He let his fingertips glide down her neck, across her noticeable collarbones, and slip to the tops of her breasts, barely touching them with his fingers. Maggie's breath caught in her throat quickly. Robert noticed this and murmured, "Ahh so the ice queen does feel." A smirk displayed upon his face rightly.

His eyes kidnapped hers once again, daring her to look away. His hand slid to the front of her tank top; his fingers landing on a button, undoing the first one on. Robert's eyes stayed locked on Maggie's watching the terror blossom to life within the deepest part of her.

"What are you doing?" questioned Maggie strangely. She stepped back, Robert's grasp tightened on her arm, his fingers digging into her flesh. Robert undid the second and the third buttons very slowly. Each time a button was undone, her breath always caught in her throat, making her chest rise slowly, but heavily. Her skin warmed at his touch.

He peeled away the pieces of her tank top and looked his fill. Maggie wriggled against the grasp his hand on her arm, but Robert didn't dare allow his hand to budge an inch. He declared strongly,

"Maggie you're so beautiful." His attention returned back to her face, his eyes drilling in hers. Maggie didn't know whether or not to accept his compliment or not.

"Well I'm sorry to report, but this is all you will be seeing for tonight." Maggie replied annoyed and batted her eyelashes a couple of times. He released his hold on her. *Hey it worked, he's such a sucker.* Maggie laughed in her throat sweetly.

She ambled up the old dirt road leaving Robert standing in a daze to ponder what just happened. Maggie swung her hips and fanny side to side. Robert regained control of his senses and trailed after her like a pup following its mom. Catching up with Maggie, Robert threw her over his shoulder and shouted, "You'll never get away from me Maggie, honey. Sorry babe."

"Robert, put me down right this instance! Got it?"

"Sure. I'll put you down." He tossed her to the ground. She landed on her butt hard. Her butt hurt, but she jumped abruptly onto his back.

He shouted, "Oh so now you want a piggy back ride?"

"Sure. Why not?" declared Maggie. She rode home all the way on his back. Once they reached the back of the house, Robert tried the door. It was still unlocked so they entered quietly and went to the room where each was to sleep. He whispered across the hall, "Goodnight, Maggie."

"Goodnight Robert." murmured Maggie unimpressed. He opened his door and slipped inside.

Maggie crept as quietly as she could into Abby's room. She changed into her pajamas by the light in the corner and hopped onto the top bunk. She closed her eyes and fell fast asleep, thinking of tonight and how naïve she had been. Robert found his bottom bunk in the dark. He slid his jeans off and ripped his shirt off over his head and then crawled under the sheet, laying his head back with ease onto the pillow. He looked at the picture on the wall and sighed. Robert fell asleep thinking of Maggie.

Chapter Four
LAYING DOWN THE LAW

"Bye Maggie dear and bye Joe. I hope you had fun!" shouted Mrs. Anderson excitedly.

"Don't worry, we did," exclaimed Maggie. She looked over at Robert shirtless, showing off his tanned, muscular six-pack chest. He smiled in amusement. She had to look away at her brother, Joe. He declared, "Well it's about time we head home and see what kind of trouble we can stir up there. What do you say?"

"Yep that seems like a plan to me," replied Maggie. They turned away, headed home down the stairs and to the driveway.

Once Maggie and Joe arrived home, they found a surprise. Their parents were sitting on the couch watching a movie together. Neither one of them knew how to accept what they were witnessing so Maggie and Joe left the living room and went to their bedrooms.

Maggie entered her room and found a card lying on the bed. She opened it up without even bothering to read the card, she opened it up and found a brand new crisp, one hundred dollar bill.

Joe strolled into her room uninvited and declared, "Did you get any money?"

"What the hell Joe? You can't just barge into my room any time you feel like it. What if I had been changing and standing without a shirt on and only a thong. I don't think you would enjoy that now, would you? I don't think so."

"Now that you mention it, that wouldn't be a good idea but now here's a question for you. What if Robert barged in uninvited, and you were almost completely naked, what would you do? Toss him out, yell at him, or let him continue his journey into your room?" After Maggie didn't reply for a whole two minutes he said, "Cat got your tongue?" He grinned and laughed uncontrollably.

Maggie answered,

"Well . . . That's none of your business anyway. I don't ask you about what you do with girls in your room for long periods of a time. Now do I?"

"That doesn't matter. We're not talking about me; we're talking about you, Maggie."

"Oh, don't worry I don't have to ask. Want to know why? I found out on my own, and I'm pretty sure we both know what you do. Don't we?" A flashback of her walking into Joe's room and stepping on a used condom proved her point. "Do I need to job your memory?"

"Shut up Maggie! Anyway you didn't answer my question about the money. Did you get any?"

"Yes I did; I got a one hundred dollar bill. How much did you get big brother?"

"Two hundred beat that Ms. Smarty-Pants."

"Ugh." Maggie stood there and rolled her eyes spitefully, placed her hand on Joe's chest, and pushed him out of her bedroom. She slammed the door shut in his face.

"Hey pass the corn to me. Stop being so mean to me Joe. You have no right." declared Alex strongly. He stood up in his chair and pointed his finger at his big brother.

"Alex honey sit down please." urged Claire. Her eyes wandered from her son, Alex standing in his seat to meeting the eyes of her husband.

"Alex! Your mother is not going to repeat herself, now please sit down at once!" demanded Dave. "Joe, please stop being a nuisance to your little brother."

"Oh come on. You know I'm just messing with you. Here you go sis!" exclaimed Joe. He put a corn on the cob on Maggie's plate, one on Alex's, and then centered the bowl on the table.

"This is such a lovely meal momma. I'm glad you cooked tonight. I was getting tired of dad's cooking," declared Alex.

"I bet you were Alex, my little baby boy," answered Mrs. Matthew's with a smile. She kissed the top of his head affectionately.

"Tomorrow we need to take the dogs to the vet Joe. So I'm going to need your assistance after breakfast."

"Yes sir," muttered Joe.

"How's everybody enjoying their meal?" asked Mrs. Matthews curiously. A smiled displayed upon her face approvingly, her eyes flipping from one child to the next.

After supper, Maggie and Joe, along with Alex went to the living room, watched a movie, and shared a bag of popcorn. They all squeezed on the mini couch and then their parents walked in. Their father, stood in front of the television, turned it off and Joe shouted at his father, "Why'd you go and do that for, huh?"

"Your father and I have decided that there need to be a few more rules. For example, you're all three going to start going to bed at ten instead of like two or three in the morning, even five sometimes," their mother said. She stared at Maggie and Joe when she spoke. They just lowered their gaze and Joe coughed flakily. "It's got to stop," declared their mom.

"Your mother is right. Rule two, computer, cells, and credit card bills. They've gotten to be too high lately." explained their father. The kids just sat there ignoring them as best as possible but without letting it show.

"Rule three, you're going to start going to some important parties, which you will have to dress really nice so you can represent us." declared Dave deeply. He looked strongly at Maggie. She lowered her head and risked a smile towards Joe who only smirked. "In addition to weddings, meetings, and lunches with me or your mother; therefore, your wardrobe is going to be changing somewhat which I've already mentioned. That was rule four.

"Rule five I came up with personally. You're going to start helping your mother around the house more. For example, cleaning, cooking, and anything else that she might need help with," explained their father.

"What . . ." shouted all the kids at once.

"Is this from that marriage counselor? Is she telling you all these things?" asked Maggie suspiciously.

"Um . . . why yes Maggie."

"Well I don't like her. Stop going!" shouted Alex stubbornly.

"Oh well geez look at the time kids. We'd really like to discuss this more but I'm afraid that it's going to have to wait until the morning," said Mr. Matthews humorously.

"Do you think that we're doing the right thing?" asked Mrs. Matthews as the kids headed up the stairs.

"Why of course, honey," answered Mr. Matthews. With that he pulled her into a tight embrace.

"I think I'll go to bed also. It's been a very long day but successful; don't get me wrong."

"I think I'll join you, my love," whispered Dave softly.

"Man I hate this. Don't you?" asked Joe.

"Well you aren't the only one." whispered Maggie loudly. She stepped into her room, jumped on her bed, and thought *I think I'll call Abby and see what she is up to.* Just as soon as Maggie called Abby, Joe snuck out the window, grabbed his skateboard, and took off down the driveway over to the old bar. Maggie stood there muttering to her self, "If he gets me into any trouble I'm going to ring his neck."

A voice popped onto the line saying, "Hello Maggie?"

"Hey Abby, what's up?"

"Not much the same old stuff like always doing laundry and cleaning, etc. I should be asking you the same question."

"Hah well wait until you hear this . . . mom and dad came up with some rules for us. Actual rules . . . do they really expect us to follow or listen to them?" Maggie glanced at her nails thinking *I need to go get my nails redone that lady messed up on my manicure.*

"What are you serious? Your parents are on crack or something hon. By the way, did your brother sneak out because my brother isn't in his room anymore; he was just in there too."

"Yes unfortunately that asshole. They probably went to the old bar, you know? So have you talked to Johnny lately?" quizzed Maggie curiously.

"Oh you know that I have."

"So, what did he say?"

"He said that he likes me like a lot and wants to take me out on a date next week. He said that I was one of the prettiest girl's that he'd ever seen," exclaimed Abby happily.

"Are you for real? That was really sweet of him to say that. So where's he going to take you, time, and what day? Well come on girl, I have to know these thing, right?"

"True, all right. Well the time is five o'clock, the day is Tuesday of next week, and he won't tell me where he's taking me because he said it's a surprise."

"Are you serious?" exclaimed Maggie threw the phone.

"Why yes. Why would I lie about something like this?"

"Oh I don't know. Well I have to go before the wardens make their rounds. Have fun alright?"

"Hang on . . . Since you and Robert are kinda hooked up, I was wondering if you could go with us too. I'm going to tell them about Johnny and have him come over to meet them, along with talking which will be a very big thing. I just hope they agree with him. You know?"

"I know. He seems like a really nice guy."

"He does, doesn't he? What about Robert? He's a great guy too!"

"Shut up. He is in some ways but in other ways he's not. Plus I have to think about my dad and what he'll say about all of this. He doesn't even agree with having Joe as his son. Yes, he might make good grades, but outside of school, he's always in trouble," replied Maggie.

"Same way with Robert too I've got to be getting off okay? Night Mag."

"Night Abby." muttered Maggie sleepily with a yawn.

Chapter Five
MURDER DOWN THE STREET

"Tell me where you have been sneaking off too, and with who?" shouted Dave.

"No, it's none of your damn business!" Joe shouted at his father.

"Don't you dare talk to me like that Joe! I think I deserve the right to know, considering I'm your *father!*"

"Of course *you're* going to think that!"

"Look, please just tell me; okay?" Mr. Matthews pleaded followed by a deep sigh. He closed his eyes wondering where he went wrong with his oldest son.

"Fine I will tell you. I've been going down to the old bar. You know the one that's been shut down for years? Well a couple of my friends and I have been going there just to hang out." answered Joe giving into his father, no longer finding the urge to fight him.

He stood there staring at his father, the worry wrinkles had deepened making Mr. Matthews look older than he really was.

"No, it's not all right. Have you been drinking?" Dave questioned, "Have you been doing drugs or smoking anything? What about your sister? Has she?"

"No she has never been there as far as I know," Joe lied. Nobody seemed to notice Maggie's blushed face, sitting on the edge of the bottom stairs until Alex lazily trotted down to Maggie.

Alex whispered sleepily, "What's going on?"

"Maggie come here please and sit down on the couch with me." Clare murmured encouragingly. "Please be a good girl. As for you Alex, go back to your room. This doesn't concern you."

Alex shrugged his shoulders and walked back to his room.

"Maggie, have you ever drunk any kind of alcohol, smoked, done drugs, or ever been to the old bar?"

"No, to every single one of those questions."

"Thank you," whispered Dave thankfully. "As for you Joe, you are grounded for a month. Got it?"

"Whatever," Joe declared, malice present within his voice directed straight for his father. He stood up and walked upstairs to his room muttering hateful things under his breath. Mr. and Mrs. Matthews heard Joe slam his bedroom door shut. Maggie rose from the couch softly, disappearing up the staircase to her room unnoticed. She pulled on light, purple cheerleading shorts, white tank top, black socks and Nike running shoes. As she walked into the bathroom, her phone began to ring. She turned around, rushing back across the hall to her bed reaching for the phone.

"Hey I have to tell you something," Abby said urgently.

Maggie leaned against the doorframe, listening to Abby explain about Robert and Johnny. She hung up; left the bathroom pulling her hair back into a tight ponytail, grabbed her I-pod, and slipped quietly downstairs and out the front door without anybody noticing her.

"Robert! Are you listening to me? Please, don't you dare have this knife throwing contest with Johnny! You're still new at it," pleaded Abby as she threw her hands to her hips angrily. The sun's violent rays descended downward, touching Abby softly, warming her skin at its simple touch.

He pulled out his four inch knife. Abby gasped, once she saw the knife, it's reflection in the sun shined across her face. Robert whispered, "Hey I'm sorry Abby. I have to do this." He threw the knife up into the air and caught it. Abby walked away into the house, slamming the door furiously behind her.

Maggie bent down to retie her shoelaces and thought *I think I'll stop by Abby's house and see how Robert and Abby are doing. Maybe she'd want to go jogging with me.* She straightened up and continued on her mile long jog to Abby's house.

"Robert you need to come inside!" shouted Abby out the back screen door. Flies fluttered around, trying their hardest to reach their destination within the house. Robert had his stereo blaring and he couldn't hear Abby. "Well since he can't hear me, I will just go to him."

Abby, hadn't noticed her brother throwing a knife up in the air. She marched right up behind him, standing but only inches apart. Abby reached out with her first two fingers, gently tapping him on the shoulder when all of a sudden, she heard a scream. She thought in wonderment, *who is screaming; am I screaming?* Seeing blackness swelling itself around her, dragging her body into that deep darkness; it felt like the world was giving out beneath her. She could feel her body shrink to the ground ever so slowly; numbness seared throughout her veins, shutting off her senses.

Maggie was twenty-five feet away from Abby's house when she heard the scream. It came from out of nowhere it seemed. And then Maggie saw what was taking place before her eyes. She stood there, transfixed, witnessing Abby lying on the ground. She saw Robert drop to his knees beside her. Maggie stood frozen in time, gazing at the scene before her until her senses returned. She ran to them, her pulse quickening rapidly as she approached. Maggie saw the knife and the blood slithering out of Abby's head, where the knife had entered. Drop after drop landed upon the hard, green covered ground forming a puddle beneath her head, surrounding Abby's head, staining her blonde hair, red.

Maggie sank to the ground beside Abby, dizzily looking at Robert then back at the knife. She saw the terrified look on his face and she knew. She screamed, a cold blood scream, freezing Robert's heart and his mind all at once; sending shivers up and down his spine.

"No! No!" then at a rush she felt somebody wrap their arms around her, drawing her body to them. By this point Maggie's eyes were swimming with tears. She looked up into Abby's dad's face through her tear covered eyes.

Abby's mom was on the ground by her daughter's head, talking rapidly on the phone. Maggie noticed how Mrs. Anderson was crying so strongly and heavily. She slid out of Mr. Anderson's arms and cat-crawled over to Mrs. Anderson, wrapping her arms around Abby's mom.

"It was him!" Maggie pointed her finger at Robert, the boy she loved like a brother, one of her best friends.

Robert sat there stunned, not able to speak or stand up for himself. The realization that Abby, his little sister was lying on the ground covered in her own blood with a knife sticking out of her head, hadn't suck in yet. He was able to murmur softly, "But I . . . I didn't do this. I couldn't have . . ."

By this time his mother was off the phone, staring at Maggie curiously asking, "Robert? It was Robert?" She looked over at her son, screaming. Mrs. Anderson got up hastily, ran into her husband's waiting arms. He embraced her.

Maggie sat by Abby's head, pulled her right hand into hers and gently squeezed it. Her hand was soft, but cold and lay dead within her own hand. She heard the sound of loud, roaring sirens of the police arriving and the ambulance; she heard yelling and shouting. Then the last thing she saw was Abby being lifted onto a long, metal stretcher, with white sheets covering her body. She felt herself lose control of the world around her, and her mind and soul slid into a deep black hole.

Chapter Six
REALITY NIGHTMARE

"Maggie. Maggie, are you awake?" Her eyes fluttered open. She saw her brightly colored walls and found herself starring into the face of her father. She sat up slowly and looked around her room. She was lying on her orange and hot pink sheets on her bed. She asked curiously, "Where's Abby? I have to see her I need to tell her that I had the weirdest, but most awful dream about her dying. The funny but scary thing was her brother had killed her," Maggie laughed unknowingly that her nightmare was real. Her parents just looked at one another, worriedly, and then glanced back at Maggie. She thought *uh oh. What's happened? Something is definitely wrong.* Then she realized what it was.

"Honey, that was no dream; Abby really is dead. You witnessed her death . . . her being murdered. Then you fainted as the police took her body away. I'm sorry, honey."

"No, you're lying! She's not dead; you have to be lying! Say that you are, oh please tell me that you're lying!" Maggie shouted desperately. She looked helplessly from her mother to her father, as it all came rushing back to her; the blood sliding from Abby's wound and the knife casting its reflection from the sun onto her face and the sound of that harsh, cold blood-curdling scream, fresh in her mind; feeling as if she were witnessing it all over again.

"Did they have any witnesses?"

"Um . . . honey, you are the only witness that the police have at the moment. You have to testify against him."

"You mean Robert? That means simply that I'm going to have to be the one that throws his ass in jail."

"Yes, honey. I'm so sorry . . . I wish that you hadn't been there." her mother wrapped her arms supportively around Maggie's body, crying silently. Maggie felt like she'd been punched in the stomach, like she was the one who had been stabbed with the knife instead of her best friend. She retreated from her mom's warm embrace and ran out of her bedroom, down the hall into the bathroom.

Dave and Clare ran her, they saw their daughter leaning over the toilet, and smelled the harsh stench of vomit. Clare reached for Maggie's hair and held it back in her fist. Dave ran a washcloth under cold water for Maggie.

Clare whispered, "I hear somebody knocking. Honey will you go see who is at the door?" Dave handed his wife the wet washcloth and ran downstairs.

Maggie leaned her head back and stared into her mom's eyes, as the waterworks started all over again. Dave quietly walked back inside,

"It's the police. They are here to question Maggie about . . . today." Dave dreaded to say anything about the current events. "The sheriff is accompanying them," he added.

"Well I'm sorry, but they're just going to have to wait to get their questions answered until another day," said Mrs. Matthews.

"They said they have to do the questioning tonight. They can't wait until tomorrow; I already asked them."

Maggie whispered weakly, "Mom . . . dad, I'm okay really; trust . . ." her next words were drowned out by her own vomit spilling itself from her mouth covering the bottom of the toilet. After hearing his daughter speak, his heart grieved for his only daughter and seeing her in so much pain made Mr. Matthews want to kill Robert personally himself.

"How about now . . . Do you think they'll do the questioning tomorrow?" Clare questioned sarcastically.

Dave left Maggie and his wife alone in the bathroom. He descended back downstairs to join the police officers. Just as he exited, Maggie pulled her head back and whispered, "I'll be fine. I promise I can do this."

"Are you sure babydoll?" Clare asked worriedly.

"I'm positive."

"Um . . . officers can we please do this questioning another night? My daughter, Maggie is upstairs lying on the bathroom floor sick," reported Dave.

"Mr. Matthews, here comes your daughter and wife right now," declared Officer Todd. Dave turned around and gave Mrs. Matthews a look that asked what's going on? Mrs. Matthews just smiled back at him. Dave thought *what in the world?*

"Maggie if you'll just take a seat here on the couch," asked Sheriff Adam calmly. He stared through his glasses at her possible questions forming to life within his mind.

Maggie sat down on the couch across from the sheriff. He pulled out a notepad and a pen along with a tape recorder. "So tell me Maggie. How old are you?"

"Twelve."

"Please tell us your full name."

"My name is Magnolia Ann Matthews."

"Good. What were you doing at Abby's house? Your parents tell us that you were supposed to be in your room or so they thought."

"I had changed into the outfit that I'm wearing right now and I decided that I needed some fresh air so I went for a jog to Abby's house thinking that maybe she would want to join me," admitted Maggie.

"Let me ask you this. What exactly did you see once you reached Ms. Anderson's house?"

"As I was walking up, I saw Robert standing there throwing a knife up in the air and I heard Abby yelling at him, but I couldn't hear what she was saying because the stereo was on. So I kept on walking. She was . . . about a few inches . . . apart from him. He had his back to her." She sniffled back some tears. Officer Tom looked at her, patted Maggie on the hand and whispered, "Take all the time you want." She nodded her head okay and continued.

"As I was saying, he had his back to her and he had thrown the knife up . . . and I guess . . . she didn't see it. Because . . . the next moment I know . . . I hear this heart crushing scream. I guess it came . . . from her. I don't remember," cried Maggie. She began a set of fresh, new tears. One of the officers standing back who was listening closely handed her a few tissues. She dried her eyes and blew her nose clutching the used tissues in her fists.

"Then I saw Abby . . . she was laying on the ground . . . her face staring up at the sky and I saw Robert drop to his knees at Abby's head. I ran over to them . . . fell to the ground . . . and once I saw the knife . . . the blood . . . it was so red and it was just coming out of her head, nonstop." The deputy had written down most of what Maggie had said but he let the tape recorder do some of the work also.

"No, she can't be dead! I can't believe it . . . she's dead, my best friend!" Maggie screamed. Her body slumped back against the couch, drew her knees up to her chest, buried her head in her legs and cried. Clare came over and wrapped her arms around Maggie. She pressed her head to her mother's shoulder and just let all the pain from today wash away.

Deputy Terry stood up and said unhappily, "Can I speak with you for a moment, Dave?" He stepped away towards the front door out of earshot. Dave walked over to him and said, "Sure." Dave stood in front of Terry and he asked, "What's the problem Dave? I saw the look that you kept giving me."

"Well when Maggie woke up she said that she'd had a dream that Abby had died and the funny thing was that Robert had killed her." Dave stared worriedly at his best friend since elementary school waiting for Terry's reply.

"You need to take her to a therapist or a psychiatrist. She needs some help Dave and you know I'm being honest with you." Dave's gaze flipped to his daughter and sighed. "We're going to go now. We have to visit the parents and we can't put it off any longer."

"Alright I understand." Dave said staring at Terry appreciating all the help that he had been tonight. Terry patted Dave on the back and murmured,

"If you need me for anything, don't hesitate to call or drop by." Dave let Terry and the other officers along with the sheriff out. As soon as they all had left, he shut and locked the door.

He headed upstairs to Maggie's room. When he stepped across the threshold, he found Maggie asleep in her bed, with her head lying in Clare's lap. Clare looked up when he entered and gave a weak smile. She slipped a pillow under her daughters' head as she stood up. She shut the light off in Maggie's room and followed her husband down to their bedroom.

Chapter Seven
POINTING FINGERS

Maggie stared outside her window, the rain beating against the glass and the strong wind whipping through the trees, thrashing the green covered limbs around the air. She rested her chin in the palm of her hand and continued staring outside. Her mind wondered, questioning things in her life, whether she was making the right decision or not. Deep down she knew that she was and knowing that, confidence blossomed within her.

"Maggie!" She turned her head towards the entrance of her bedroom the mention of her name. Clare stood at the threshold, her face red and fists clenched, dangling at her side.

"Yes?" Maggie questioned gloomily.

"Are you almost ready? So we can leave and get this over with?"

"Yes mom," murmured Maggie.

"Thank God!" She turned on her heel and stormed down the hall, this time hollering for her brother, Joe. Her dad, Dave stood there this time, watching his daughter, trying to figure out how this happened to Maggie, his baby girl.

"Hey dad," She smiled weakly. He walked over to her and sat down on the couch next to her. He stared out the window, his eyes seeing the outside world differently than what Maggie was seeing. They sat there in silence watching the outside world transform before them. Knowing that neither one of them could do anything, but Maggie knew that she could make a difference today.

Dave placed his hand atop Maggie's and squeezed gently. Their eyes met locking upon each other, for a few seconds nothing seemed to matter, but only this moment being shared between father and daughter. They returned their attention to the windows, gazing out beyond the glass. The sharp sound of heels hitting the hardwood floor alerted their senses. Clare's voice disrupted the peaceful silence.

"It's time." Dave's gaze turned back to Maggie and he whispered,

"Here it goes." He stood up, straightening his black, suit jacket and walked over to join his wife downstairs. Maggie took one last look outside and stood up, rubbing her hands up and down her dress, straightening the kinks out.

Maggie sat in the witness seat, her heart racing. Her gaze kept flickering back and forth from face upon face, only recognizing a select few. She was still having trouble believing that yes, she Maggie Matthews sat in the front of a courtroom.

The air was thick and smothering. She kept telling herself to just breathe normal and things will be fine. Mrs. Tanner, the prosecuting attorney stood before Maggie in a clean cut suit that probably costs her a good couple hundred bucks. She stared at Maggie intensely. Her voice rang out across the silent courtroom, directed to her only.

"Is this person, the boy who you saw murder Ms. Abby Anderson?" Mrs. Tanner turned and pointed her finger at Robert sitting in the seat next to the defense attorney. Maggie didn't even need to look at him, she already knew.

"Yes ma'am," Maggie answered strongly.

"Did the boy you see have a tattoo?"

"Yes ma'am."

"What kind of tattoo?" Mrs. Tanner asked.

"A cobra curling up his arm and it starts at his hand, curling all the way up his arm and over his shoulder," Maggie replied confidence surging within her veins.

"Here is a picture of the tattoo on Robert Anderson's arm. Is this the same tattoo that you saw?" questioned the prosecuting attorney.

"Yes ma'am."

"Thank you and I have no further questions your honor." declared Mrs. Tanner.

"Would the defense like to re-cross examine the witness?"

"Yes your honor." Maggie glanced at Robert. She saw him smiling very confidently. She directed her attention to the defense attorney, Mr. Clay steadily walking her way.

"Abby was your best friend, wasn't she?"

"Yes sir."

"Now don't you have a crush on my client?" Mr. Clay asked, a smirk displayed across his clean shaved face.

"No sir; not anymore." declared Maggie, smiling sweetly at Mr. Clay. *Yeah, you just try and get to me because your games aren't going to work.*

"Hmm . . . now why would that be?"

"Because he murdered my best friend and the girl that was like my sister," Maggie spat spitefully at Mr. Clay.

"Now then you were there the day Abby was murdered weren't you?" Maggie glanced towards Robert and answered strongly,

"Yes as a matter of fact I was."

"Why were you there may I ask?"

"Simple. I was out for a jog and I wanted to stop by and see if Abby wanted to go jogging with me. Abby and I were jogging partners," replied Maggie.

"I see . . . Do you carry a knife around with you by any chance?" Maggie thought *he's trying to swing the case to look like I did it.* She answered sweetly,

"Yes, but only when I go the drag strip." The defense attorney's smile slid from his face as Maggie answered.

"Okay," Mr. Clay murmured to himself. He spun out another question that he hoped would catch her answering wrongly, but his hopes faded.

"Did you and Abby ever get into any arguments or fights?" *Oh he is such a jerk . . . he's trying to get me to say the wrong thing and make myself look like a huge fool in front of everybody, but sorry it isn't going to happen.*

"No sir, not ever." Maggie smiled sweetly at Mr. Clay. The defense attorney's hopes died. He knew he couldn't make her look like the bad guy so he decided to try the next witness. Maggie sat there watching the man, his facial expressions changing.

"Thank you, no further questions your honor." Mr. Clay strolled away and dropped himself back into his seat heavily next to Robert.

"Would the prosecution like to re-cross examine the witness?" questioned the judge.

"Yes your honor." exclaimed Mrs. Tanner. She stood up ready to end this case and throw Mr. Anderson behind bars where he rightly belonged. Maggie glanced from Mrs. Tanner to her parents and smiled slowly back at them.

"Ms. Matthews, why do you think Robert would want to kill his sister? What possible motive could he have to perform this horrible act?" Nothing could have prepared Maggie for this question. She inhaled a deep breath and answered.

"Abby told me when Joe and I had stayed the night at their house on May 26 she had snuck up on Robert while he was reading his email and scared him. She screamed 'ah' at him and Robert jumped out of his seat. Then Abby said something about how Robert started yelling and shouting at her," she took a deep breath continuing. "As Robert was sitting back in his chair, Abby read his email and she confronted Robert about his drinking habits. Abby told me that he got extremely mad. She told me that he made the comment that if she told their mom, he was going to snitch on her about Johnny and Robert supposedly tried choking her."

Silence consumed the courtroom, an occasional cough or heavy breathing but Maggie locked eye contact with Robert. He gazed back at her intensely, daring her to say more. Maggie knew she was speaking the truth. Mrs. Tanner smiled confidently and turned her attention back to Maggie.

"Thank you, your honor. I have no further questions." Mrs. Tanner stepped away from the witness stand and walked back to her seat, standing and waiting patiently.

"If the prosecution has no further questions, the witness may step down from the stand." declared the Judge loudly. Maggie walked away from the witness stand feeling numb. She sat down beside Mrs. Tanner and glanced at her attorney. She smiled at Maggie and returned her attention back to the judge.

"I'd like to call Johnny McCall as my next witness." Johnny stood up slowly, walked to the stand, and placed his right hand on the bible. The Bailiff standing next to the witness stand, holding the bible asked.

"Do you swear to tell the truth, the whole truth, and nothing but the truth?"

"Yes sir."

"The witness may be seated at this time," declared the Judge. Johnny sat calmly before his family, friends, and the entire courtroom. The prosecuting attorney stood up relaying questions to him.

"Please state your name."

"Johnny McCall."

"How old are you?"

"Sixteen."

"Did you know Abby?"

"Yes ma'am."

"What was your relation with Abby?"

"Girlfriend." Johnny whispered softly.

"I see . . ." murmured Mrs. Tanner. "Were you and Robert going to have a knife throwing contest?"

"Yes ma'am. Robert confronted me about it. He said that if I won, I got to date Abby. If he won, I had to stop seeing Abby." Johnny's gaze flickered from Robert, to me, back to Robert. He allowed his gaze to linger a few seconds longer on Robert.

"Where were you on the day of Abby's murder?" questioned Mrs. Tanner.

"I was at work."

"Where do you work?"

"Southern States."

"Thank you. No further questions at this time your honor." Mrs. Tanner said strongly.

"Would the defense attorney like to question the witness?"

"Yes ma'am." Mr. Clay stood up asking, "Johnny you said you work at Southern States; therefore, how far of a drive is it from Abby's house to your work?"

"I'd say about thirty, maybe forty minutes. Why?"

"Just wondering; thank you, your honor and I have no further questions." Mr. Clay walked back to his seat and smiled at Robert.

"Would the prosecution like to re-cross examine the witness?" Johnny's gaze flipped from his parents to Maggie and smiled, reminding her about what they talked about before the trial.

"Yes, your honor," declared Mrs. Tanner. She tugged on her suit jacket and asked, "When did your shift end that day? When was the contest going to take place?" The prosecuting attorney walked up to him and stood waiting for an answer.

"My shift wasn't over until four o' clock. The contest was going to take place at four-thirty or around five."

"Thank you. I have no further questions, your honor."

"Then the witness may step down."

Johnny stepped down, walked over to Maggie and sat next to her, letting out a slow breath. The prosecuting attorney stood up. Her chair scraped the marbled floor, hitting the railing behind her. She declared, "I'd like to call Robert Anderson to the stand."

Robert stood up smiling and walked to the stand approaching the Bailiff, with a smirk spread across his face. He sat lazily in the chair, sitting before Mrs. Tanner still smirking.

"Robert, what were you doing on the day of Abby's murder?" asked Mrs. Tanner smirking.

"I was listening to Three Days Grace and throwing my knife up in the air." Mrs. Tanner nodded her head in approval.

"Why were you throwing your knife up in the air?" Robert glanced from the prosecuting attorney to Maggie and replied.

"I was getting ready for the knife throwing contest with Johnny." He never took his gaze off Maggie. Again Mrs. Tanner nodded her head in agreement, listening.

"Is it true, about what Johnny said? You had confronted him to have the knife throwing contest?"

"Yes ma'am every word of it." His gaze returned to Mrs. Tanner and he sat there thinking *Gosh, come on and hurry up with all of these damn questions!*

The prosecuting attorney, paced back and forth, until finally deciding on the right question to ask, "Okay, is it true that you have a temper?"

"Yes ma'am, I won't deny it." Robert squirmed in his seat thinking *oh shit. She's asking the deep questions.*

"Hmm . . . do you drink alcohol?" Her gaze locked on him penetrating that tough boy act. He sneered at Mrs. Tanner and returned his gaze back to Maggie.

"Were you mad at Abby for wanting to tell your mom about you drinking again?"

"Yes ma'am." Mrs. Tanner stopped and stood directly in front of the witness stand saying,

"I bet you were, weren't you? Thank you and that's all, your honor. I'm through questioning the witness." She stepped back from the witness stand and sat in her seat confidently.

The judge declared, "Would the defense like to question Robert Anderson?"

"Yes your honor."

"You admit to drinking. What was it again that you were drinking?"

"I usually drink beer, whiskey, and vodka."

"Were you drinking at the time of your sister's death?"

"Yes sir." Robert squirmed in his seat wondering what his attorney was getting at.

"Thank you and that is all, your honor. I have no further questions." Mr. Clay said weakly, walking back to his seat.

"Would the prosecution like to re-cross examine the witness at this time?"

"Yes your honor." Mrs. Tanner stood up facing Robert. "Robert, you say you were drinking. Drinking what? The cops tested you, your alcohol level wasn't that high."

"Yes ma'am. I was only drinking beer."

"Okay." murmured Mrs. Tanner. "You weren't under the influence so what happened? What made you snap Robert?" Mrs. Tanner continued standing before Robert, smiling.

"I don't know what happened. I just threw my knife up in the air and then I heard this scream. That scream woke my insides up. It froze my blood where I was standing. I guess you could say that I was standing. I guess you could say that I was like in a daze. I was just so mad at her, so mad. I remember thinking I could've killed her."

Maggie sat in silence watching the scene take place before her. She couldn't believe what she was hearing. A few stray tears trickled down Robert's face.

"Thank you and I have no further questions your honor." Mrs. Tanner declared confidently knowing that she had sealed the deal, and she had won her case.

"Would the defense like to re-cross examine the witness?"

"No, your honor," answered Mrs. Clay. His face held a defeated look.

"The witness may step down." Robert wiped away his tears and walked slowly back to this seat, taking his place beside the defense attorney, Mr. Clay, smirking.

"The court will take a recess while the jury deliberates on the final sentence," shouted the judge. She slammed her gavel down on the desk and stepped down.

Chapter Eight
FINAL WORD

Maggie sat by Johnny and held his hand, waiting to hear the verdict, to hear whether Robert was guilty or innocent. In her heart she knew he was guilty, plain and simple, but it depends all on the jury. She allowed her gaze to land upon Robert. He sat still, smirking and watching her. Johnny squeezed her hand as the Judge returned to her seat, sitting before the courtroom declaring,

"The Jury has come to the conclusion and understanding that the sentence of Robert Anderson is guilty to the First Degree of Murder," Maggie sat there, her attention turned to Robert. Two cops stood next to Robert, urging him to stand. He stood, turned, and smiled at Maggie as the officers slapped handcuffs on his wrists. The two cops led him away into another room.

Maggie stood up and her parents reached for her, giving her a hug and a kiss. The prosecuting attorney shook hands with everybody there that she was representing. Maggie sat back down in her seat, her vision blurring with tears, closing her eyes and saying a silent prayer for Abby.

"Come on honey, your plane leaves at noon today. We need to leave. Now!" hollered Dave up the stairs. Maggie came down wearing a yellow sundress. Her hair dyed a caramel brown with blonde highlights; she wore white heels as she trotted down the stairs to her father.

"How do I look?"

"Different," exclaimed Alex, her little brother. Joe looked at Maggie then at their dad, wondering what just in the hell and happened.

"You look beautiful sweetie." Dave walked up to his daughter and gave her a bear hug, which drained her breath. She gasped for air as he planted her feet back on the hardwood floor. Dave strolled, his daughter outside, Joe and Alex followed suit, getting in their father's Escalade.

As they were pulling out of the driveway, Maggie exclaimed, "I wish mom was here so she could see me off too."

"I know pumpkin, but things just didn't work out between your mother and me. We may have been going to marriage counseling, but we were too deep in our relationship already and counseling couldn't help us. We tried kids, we really did. She still loves you, you know that right? We may be getting a divorce but eventually everything will turn out for the best." replied Mr. Matthews.

Maggie turned around in her seat and stared out the window, gazing at the house that she'd been living in since she was brought home from the hospital. She turned around and smiled to herself until she remembered Robert, what he had told her. Maggie couldn't help but wonder if he would be back or not.

Chapter Nine

THE OLD FRIEND

Heat from the sun's rays reached down upon Maggie, caressing her skin with its violent fingers. She wiped the back of her tanned arm across her forehead, brushing the beads of sweat away. She sat thinking *I can't believe it's been six years since Abby's death . . . six years. It's still so hard to imagine and the face that I've been living in Georgia, the whole time. At least I'm used to my new name, Megan Johnson.*

"Megan! Why aren't you planting those flowers like I told you to do?" yelled Nana out the front the door. "Stop staring at those hot boys and put your tongue back in your mouth. You're drooling all over my flower beds. I'm not growing drool lilies ya know!"

"Yes Nana!" shouted Megan furiously. She rolled her eyes at hearing this complain. The two boys walked on past her. They kept turning their heads and gazing back at Megan. The cuter of the two, whispered something to the tall, red-haired boy. Her gaze dropped lower from their muscled, broad shoulders to the swagger of their tightly, fitted jeans.

"When you get done, come on inside so you can eat lunch!" hollered Nana. "Megan I'm not going to tell you again to put your tongue back in your mouth. It looks like a red carpet hanging from your face." Megan leaned back, sitting on her butt, raised her hands up in defeat murmuring,

"Nana, why did you have to embarrass me? Gosh that tall dirty blonde headed boy was gorgeous. Nana, you ruined my moment." When she heard her best friend's mom yelling at her son, Megan thought *he's probably in trouble or didn't do something that she probably told him days ago to do.*

"Bryan, come on! You have your orthodontist appointment at eleven o' clock!"

"All right Mom, I'm coming! Just wait till I say bye to Megan," Bryan yelled to his mother. He ran across the green lawn to his cousin. "Bye Megan. Are we still going to the creek along with the rest of the guys later?"

"Yes! It's like ninety-eight degrees out here and it's only ten o' clock," answered Megan with a smile. When Megan saw Bryan jump into his mom's white '08 mustang along with his little sister Krissy, Megan hurriedly planted the last flower. She stared at her handiwork and nodded in approval. After putting away all the tools she had been using, she ran through the garage connecting to the kitchen and sat down at the kitchen table.

"Your father called and said that your brother, Alex and him, won't be home for at least another two or three days."

"Remind me again where they went?" commented Megan.

"Remember they went on a camping and hiking trip; some father and son bonding trip."

"Oh yeah that's right," said Megan uninterested and ready to off the subject, remembering that her father didn't do anything like that with her anymore. Nana patted Megan's hand and hobbled outside to the front lawn to check on the flowers that Megan had planted.

Megan finished eating and left the kitchen for her bedroom upstairs. She changed out of her dirty work clothes into a bikini. She threw on a pair of dark blue shorts and a white tank top. Looking at herself in the dresser mirror, she stood admiring her long blonde hair, thinking *I wish I had the heart to cut my hair but I know that I don't.*

She shrugged her shoulders and headed back downstairs to sit outside on the porch. Megan turned her head and watched the car creep along slowly down the street. The shiny, recently restored, cherry red 1969 Chevy Chevelle stopped in front of Nana's house. She could feel goose bumps forming on her skin even though it was almost a hundred degrees outside.

Megan knew just about every vehicle on the street but not this particular car. The driver within the car rolled down the window slowly intriguing Megan even more. The driver was a man was about nineteen or twenty which she knew deep down she had seen him somewhere before, but she couldn't think of when or where, and it made her nervous.

The man pulled out a cigarette and Megan sat watching him lift his hand to light it. She saw the tattoo of a cobra on the back of his hand crawling up his arm, disappearing under his shirt. Megan whispered, "I've seen that same tattoo on another guy's arm before, but whom?"

She continued staring intensely at the man, still dumbfounded. The driver of the car turned his head slowly and locked his gaze upon Megan. Butterflies swarmed to life within her stomach making Megan nervous. She jumped up running back inside, but before shutting the door, she turned around and saw him still sitting there. He was smiling and gazing at her with a long, hard look of desire; his eyes roaming curiously over her body. She slammed the door shut, blocking his wandering eyes from view. Megan locked the door and threw herself onto the couch.

Then it dawned on her; she knew who it was. "Its' the guy that turned my world upside down," murmured Megan. "It was Robert Anderson." She sat up abruptly, her heart beating rapidly within her chest. The shrill sound of a ringing broke the silence surrounding Megan. She finally answered it hearing a deep, husky voice murmur, "I'm back."

The line clicked dead, erupting within its place, surrounding her. She sat there staring at the phone. Finally, she dropped the phone atop the table. "It was Robert." Fear stormed to life, twisting throughout Megan. She ran upstairs to her room, turning on the radio wanting to be surrounded by voices, no longer empty silence. Nana stepped into her room asking sweetly,

"I'm going into town. Want to join me?"

"Um no, I'm sorry Nana." Megan glanced quickly at her bed avoiding her grandmother's stare.

"Oh yeah I forgot. Bryan and you along with the rest of the guys are going to the creek later." said Nana.

"Yes."

"Well if you go, don't forget to lock the doors."

"Okay," answered Megan.

The sun beat on his bare back as he sat by the water, watching the ripples form as the water roamed over the rocks. Robert stared at the leaves strolling along the surface, watching them float further down the stream. He whispered to himself, "Maggie, sweet Maggie. What am I going to do with you?" Robert flicked his cigarette bud in the water, gazing deeply, his thoughts consumed of Maggie, his Maggie.

Megan sat heavily on the swing. "Let's see here he was fourteen when he left and it's been six years. I'm sixteen now, so Robert would have to be about twenty." She skimmed her fingers through her hair, pulling it over her shoulder, "I wonder what he thinks of me?" *Whoa . . . wait just one minute. Why in the hell am I thinking that for? Why should I care what he thinks about me?*

The still air allowed the heat to form a blanket within the air, suffocating Megan. The shade from the porch only offered the slightest amount of relief. Thoughts of the cold, water from the creek caressing her tanned, hot skin chilled her senses. She closed her eyes and leaned against the back of the swing. A voice summoned her from her thoughts, dragging her back to reality.

"Megan! Hey, anybody in there?" asked Bryan as he waved his hands repeatedly in front of his best friends face.

"Oh what?" asked Megan.

"Are you ready to go to the creek now?" exclaimed Bryan.

"Duh!" Megan replied anxiously. "Hey lock the front door!" She stood waiting for Bryan on the lawn. He said,

"I already did!" Bryan joined Megan and as they turned the corner of the house, Melissa, William, Andrew, Chris, Allie, and Michael stopped walking, huge grins spread across their faces. Bryan declared excitedly, "Hey. Are ya'll ready to go?"

"Yes," said Allie sweetly, eyeing Bryan secretly.

Clouds drifted lazily over Robert's head, the dry heat, smothering his thoughts, drugging his blood, not wanting to do anything but lay there in peace and quiet. He laid there on the ground watching the clouds overhead. He breathed in deeply, exhaling slowly, closing his eyes in sweet serenity. His eyes flashed open upon hearing voices drift closer his way. He sat up and reached for his boots and black t-shirt lying beside him. Robert rushed behind bushes waiting for his unexpected company to arrive.

"Hey. Look we're here!" shouted Bryan. He stood by the edge of the creek. He glanced at Megan and his friends saying excitedly, "Who's ready to join me?" Bryan took his shirt off and shoes tossing them to the side. He jumped in, the cold water engulfing his body. Rest of the boys followed Bryan's example, scrambling into the creek to join him. However, Melissa, Megan, and Allie needed persuasion.

"Hey, come on! Quit being girls and jump in like a man," declared William. He started beating his fists against his chest and laughing. That did it. The girls shook off their shoes and tossed their shirts and shorts to join the rest of the pile. They jumped in to join the boys.

Robert stood behind the bushes watching the teens swim and laugh. His heart quickened at the sound of her voice, Maggie's voice. "She will always be Maggie to me though." He murmured softly. Slipping on his boots and shirt, he turned around and headed back for the suburbs. He thought *I wonder if Maggie's house is unlocked.* He sneered happily to himself, walking carefully back down the trail. "Wouldn't be a great surprise when she comes back home and finds me?" He laughed deep in his throat, excitement rushing throughout his body

As the sun was starting to disappear below the horizon, Megan, Bryan, and the rest of their friends' climbed out of the water and gathered their belongings and rushing home. Megan walked barefoot up the porch steps and watched Bryan as he waved at her before disappearing through the front door. She smiled happily to herself. She tried the front door and finding it unlocked, pissed Megan off but scared her at the same time. She shouted,

"Damn Bryan! He didn't lock the fucking door." She pushed the door in and walked to the kitchen turning a light on. Little did Megan know a surprise awaited her. A note lay by the coffee maker on the white marble counter from Nana telling her that she went to Wednesday night bingo with friends. Another note laid next to the first one nothing but a number, no name. "Let's find out who you are," said Megan with a smile.

She dialed the number, a distant ringing of a cell phone called out to her. Time stopped it seemed for Megan. "Was that my phone or . . ." Her voice trailed off, a heavy silence hung in the air-conditioned house. The ringing stopped, the last ring echoing within her ears. Her heart rate quickened, she wanted to run but she was frozen to the spot. A voice called out softly,

"Oh Maggie . . . where are you?" She looked behind her, nobody was there. Fear entrapped Megan to the spot. The strange voice called out again, but louder this time. "Oh Maggie . . ." Thoughts raced through her mind, *its' getting closer. I have to get out of here.*

Megan ran out the front door into the hot, night air. She ran into somebody, making her fall to the ground. Bryan's voice declared, "Megan? What in the hell are you doing?" She picked herself up off the ground and she mumbled loudly,

"It's Robert! He is in my house! He was in the kitchen with me!"

"What . . ." asked Bryan worriedly. He jolted past Mean into the house flipping on the living room and kitchen lights seeing nobody. "Are you positive Meg?"

"Yes I'm positive!" she shouted furiously. Megan stood right behind Bryan, her senses alerted and ready. Her eyes flickered around the room, watching.

"Megan . . . You're fine because there is nobody here." Bryan turned and stared at Megan, worried. She stared back at him in disbelief. Megan explained about the phone number she called and about how she heard it ringing and the voices.

"I called you Megan. You probably heard your own phone ringing."

"Look I will show you the piece of paper with the number on it." Megan walked over to the kitchen counter and searched it, but didn't find the paper.

"Oh no . . . No! Where is it? Bryan I swear to you that it was laying right here!" Megan whined loudly. "You don't believe me to you?"

"No." answered Bryan staring at Megan in disbelief.

"Then leave! I don't need your help anyways."

"Fine!"

"Fine!" shouted Megan angrily. Bryan turned and stormed out the front door. Megan slammed it behind him and yelled, "Damn it!"

Stars blazed down upon Robert as he stayed close to the shadows of the woods. He walked slowly watching and listening for any strange noises. His car sat parked hidden from view. He laughed to himself thinking about how easy it was to sneak in and sneak out. Robert approached his car and slid inside. He sat in the driver seat, turning his old Three Days Grace cd on. He glanced at the windows of Megan's bedroom and smiled as he watched her lights fade away to a small, hardly noticeable flicker.

His face held a smirk and slung his arm outside the window, while his other hand lightly tapped his fingers on the steering wheel in beat to the music. *I could call or text her now that I got her cell phone number.* Robert started his car and crept down the street, slowing down as he passed Maggie's house, his Maggie.

Chapter Ten
A FATHER'S WISH

"Let me guess, my loving and caring father put you up to this? I bet he asked you to get me a dress and to make sure that I wear one for him, am I right?" asked Megan, groaning like it was the end of the world.

"Yes, little missy you are right but that isn't the point." Nana replied knowingly. She continued to grin at her granddaughter even as Megan rolled her eyes. "Now I'm going to get a shower and get all prettied up. I advise you do the same my dear." Nana stood staring at Megan, warning her don't run off and hide like she normally does.

Megan mumbled, "Yes, Nana I promise to still be here waiting for you." She locked her gaze on Bryan's house, watching him leave with some chick she didn't know. Her Nana left, shutting the door softly behind her and leaving Megan alone to ponder and dwell in her thoughts.

The sun rose higher as time passed, smothering the life below the clouds in a blanket of heat. Megan left the outside world, returning back inside to the well air-conditioned house. She entered her room to find a white skirt and neon blue strapless top lying on her bed. She grinned, already knowing what she wanted to wear. Megan stood in the living room waiting patiently for Nana to finish getting ready. She stepped back into the heat, sitting on the wooden bench that her recent grandpa had made for her.

Footsteps approaching Megan alerted her. She turned to see who it was and it was none other than Robert, himself. She ducked down, thankfully watching him walk past her without a glance.

Nana stepped out onto the porch asking, "Are we ready to go to the mall?"

"Yes." Megan answered hastily. She followed her grandmother to the car quickly, ready to leave and get the fact that Robert was back out of her mind.

Robert looked over his shoulder, watching them speed away past him. He turned around, walking slowly in the direction of Nana's house, smiling devilishly to himself liking his new plan of action.

A spaghetti strap dress hung on a rack next to her, achieving her gaze. It was a solid angel white, glittering silver covering the breasts. Megan plucked it off the rack, showing it her grandmother.

"Got try it on," Nana urged excitedly.

Megan stepped out of the dressing room, standing before the full length mirror liking her reflection. She gasped saying, "It fits in all the right places." The dress hugged her breasts, tugged at her slim waist, flowing out around her hips.

"Nana I want it!"

"You do?" questioned Nana with amazement. Her eyes grew slightly, lighting up with excitement.

"Yes!" Megan exclaimed happily. She changed back into her normal clothes and joined her grandmother at the register to pay for the dress n heels. They left the store heading for the parking lot. Megan wondered what Robert was doing.

The white marble countertops gleamed at Robert. He smiled to himself soaking in the moment of being inside the house where Megan was living, his Megan. He closed his eyes, chest rising and falling. Peace settling over him as thoughts raced through his mind of Megan . . . his Maggie consumed him, drowing his mind.

As Nana parked her Ford Explorer in the driveway, a young man walked out onto the porch and Megan immediately reacted. It was Robert. He stopped dead in his tracks when he saw Megan. Robert started walking in Megan's direction exclaiming,

"Maggie!" He stepped towards her easily, stretching out his arms.

"Excuse me . . . don't you dare call me that." yelled Megan hatefully. "You know damn well that's not my name anymore, Robert!"

"Wow . . . you're actually talking to me, when I thought you wouldn't." Robert declared sarcastically, adding a smile. Megan turned away from him walking up the lawn to the house quickly. He reached for Megan's hand, grasping it in his own. She spitefully yanked her hand away, not wanting any physical contact with him.

"Don't you dare touch me either." mumbled Megan.

Robert whispered angrily, "If that's how you want to play . . . two can play this game." He followed her inside. "You're still mad at me, aren't you Maggie?"

"No! I have told you already don't call me Maggie." She threw her hands up in the air frustrated, muttering "I give up!"

"Yes you are . . . you still blame me don't you?" Robert declared with a grin. He crossed his arms over his broad chest drawing Megan's attention.

"How do you know what my feelings are?" Huh? You haven't been here with me, have you?" yelled Megan, resenting her remark. She bit her tongue, mentally yelling at herself.

"Well no! I would be if you hadn't put me away in that school!" shouted Robert.

"If you hadn't been throwing that knife around when I was walking by, then I wouldn't have seen . . ."

"It's not entirely my fault. I didn't see my sister behind me while I was throwing it!" yelled Robert. He stood only a few inches from Megan, tempted to just grab her and wrap her into his arms, but decided against it.

"Yes it is! You didn't catch it!" Megan commented over her shoulder as she walked into the kitchen. Robert followed like a pup, wandering around waiting for her next move.

"No it's not!" shouted Robert. When she turned around, her hair whipped him in the face. Tears streamed down her cheeks, making Robert feel guilty. He wrapped his arms around her murmuring gently in her ear, "Fine, I did see my sister behind me . . . I didn't mean it Maggie . . . I'm sorry, Maggie. You know that I am."

"Duh of course you didn't make it or otherwise Abby would still be here to this day with us. So was it an accident or not?'

Robert stepped back releasing Megan and answered sharply, "You know that it was an accident Maggie!" He stood in place, staring into Megan's eyes.

"How in the hell did I wind up in your arms?" questioned Megan ignoring Robert's comment.

"Hmm . . . I don't know. Maybe you're just attracted to me like that." Robert cocked his eyebrow, playing coy. Megan pushed Robert away from her, not wanting to be in his arms.

"Hey out of curiosity, would you like to go for a ride in my new car?"

"You know I can't and besides I don't think I really want to Robert." murmured Megan. "Besides you know my dad would probably shoot you. He pretty much hates you Robert."

"Oh okay." muttered Robert hurt shining deep within his eyes.

"Maybe I could go to a bar or out to eat sometime with you but just as friends, understand?"

"Yes!"

Nana broke the silence. "If you are planning on going anywhere this afternoon, remember to lock the front door on ya'lls way out, okay?" Her gaze shifted from Megan to Robert and back.

"Oh don't worry I will definitely lock the front door to keep wandering, strangers out." She glared at Robert hoping that she got the point across knowing deep down in her gut that it was him who had been lurking around her house. "But don't worry we aren't going anywhere because Robert was just leaving, weren't you?"

"Megan, you know damn well that I'm not leaving, I don't plan on going anywhere for a very long time," replied Robert. He grasped her arm squeezing so tightly that Megan gasped in pain.

Nana said, "Well okay but whatever you two decide to do, be safe."

"Okay," whispered Megan through clenched teeth.

Nana made her leave shutting the door behind her making Robert look at Megan filled with fury whispering sharply, "We're leaving right now."

"But I . . ." Megan's eyes stared back at him in disbelief.

"Don't even say a word. It will only make matters worse for you," Robert muttered dramatically. He kept his hold on Megan as they stepped out into the dry heat.

Megan's friends stood across the lawn watching Megan pull his hand off her arm, running for the safety of the house. Robert dove after Megan, wrapping his fist around her ankle making her fall to the ground. He stood up dragging her body back to him. Robert picked Megan up carrying her body to his car and tossing her inside. He drove down the street with Megan glaring at him.

She whispered, breaking the empty silence. "I'm sorry."

"What? I'm the one that should be apologizing to you but I'm not. I don't have anything to say I'm sorry for." Robert declared hatefully. He stopped at a red light and peered at Megan, noticing fear in her blazing, forget me not blue eyes. The light changed back to green making Robert's attention switch back to the road. He stole a glance at her, his Maggie. He admired Megan, loving the way her hair fell around her shoulders. The little freckles displayed cutely surrounding her cheeks and nose.

Megan's sharp voice ripped fuzzily through the silence. "Robert! Get back on your side of the road!" He flipped his head forward, seeing a car driving straight for them. Megan glared at him as she crossed her arms, turning her head away so she was staring out the window, watching the scenery whizz past her.

He looked directly at Megan and asked in an icy tone, "I hope this is okay for you." A McDonald's sign hung overhead looming at her.

"Its fine," mumbled Megan.

"Good," grunted Robert. He stepped outside, slamming the door shut behind him leaving Megan alone in his car. She scanned the parking lot, spotting her dad. She ducked down in her seat, hoping that he didn't recognize her. The driver side door opened revealing Robert holding a bag of food. Robert stared at Megan wondering what in the hell she was doing. She answered his curious stare.

"My dad is right across the street and I think he saw me."

Robert immediately focused his gaze on Megan's dad, seeing him talking to some woman. He drove away, quickly glancing back across the street and saw Mr. Johnson eyeing his car suspiciously as Robert wove his car in and out of traffic.

As they approached Nana's house, a car sat waiting for them. "Fuck! I hope to hell this isn't your father." The driver side door swung open, Megan prayed that it was him, but disappointment surged throughout her.

Joe stood there, hollering, "Hey Robert!"

"Well hells bells, look who the fuck it is! What have you been up too?" Robert climbed out of the car walking to Joe.

"Oh the usual stuff a bad ass boy does."

"I understand. So what are you doing here? I thought you lived with that one chick, damn what's her name?" He stared at Joe, his long time best friend.

"Which one?" questioned Joe. He smirked, laughing at Robert saying, "I'm just kidding. I'm still living with Tammy. I'm here because ole poppy called me wanting me to check on little ole sister, Megan here. He thought he had seen her with you." Joe glanced at Megan still sitting in the passenger seat saying, "But I'm going to tell ole poppy that Megan was not with you."

"Oh man that sounds good to me," said Robert laughing.

"Well hey I better run back to work before I get fired and I get ole miss Tammy jumping down my throat."

"Okay."

"But hey maybe we can hang out tonight?"

"Hell yes. I'll supply the beer . . ."

"And I'll bring the women," Joe replied laughing, giving Robert the double thumbs up.

He hollered humorously, "Bye, Robert."

"Bye, see you later Joe." Joe waved his hand in departure as he backed out the driveway, leaving Robert and Megan alone.

He sprang the door open, grabbing Megan by the arm, demanding. "Come on." She grabbed the food and he pulled her up the front lawn. He slammed the door shut behind him with his boot and followed Megan into the kitchen, watching the sway of her hips, creating a rhythmic pattern when she walked.

He sat down beside Megan at the counter thinking *nobody is here . . . I could get away with whatever I want. I wonder . . . should I try or wait?*

"Would you like to be friends again?" *Work slowly up the ladder then rip it out from under her once I get her where I want her.*

It took a Megan a moment to answer. "I don't know Robert . . . you know that things are different between us now since Abby's death." He continued to sit there and listen, thinking to himself. *Do I just forget all about her or what do I do? I can't because Maggie haunts my dreams, hell even my fantasies all mostly about her. She belongs to me . . . with me. Maggie is mine and nobody else's. No matter what happens I need to stay a part of her life.*

He got up suddenly and threw his trash away saying, "I guess we can try to be friends but it's going to feel weird for awhile to be honest with you. It feels awkward right now, sitting here talking to you."

"Yeah I guess I understand what you're saying. Well I better be going before your dad comes back home and sees my car in ya'lls driveway."

"That might be a good idea I'm not going to lie. The moment my dad figures out that it's your car, I have no doubt in my mind that he wouldn't think twice about putting a bullet in your head."

"You're telling me."

"Get out of here." Megan said humorously. She walked Robert to the door making sure that she locked it behind him. Before Robert left, he ran his fingers through Megan's silky, long blonde hair, and closed his eyes.

He murmured, "So soft . . ." He couldn't resist the temptation anymore. Robert placed his above Megan's head and pushed his body against hers crushing her body beneath the door and his body, pressing his well hardened manhood against her stomach.

Megan pried her mouth open allowing Robert to slide his tongue into her mouth, thoughts rushing through her head if she was making the right decision or not. When the tip of their tongues touched . . . it was like a firecracker set off, the sparks struck her jaws, pushing them to mold against Robert's own warm, gentle lips. She slid her arms around Robert's neck and shoulders, allowing her fingers to intertwine pressing against his neck, motioning for him to deepen the kiss. He moaned softly thinking *this is what I have been waiting for forever. She tastes so intoxicating I don't want to stop kissing her. I wonder what it feels like to touch that golden, light brown skin of hers.*

His hands skimmed down the length of her body bringing them back up to grasp hold of Megan's small, tiny slim waist. Megan willed herself to free her hands from Robert. Her clothes lay upon her skin wrinkled, her hair tousled, and her lips all wet and pouty. Robert's hands found her shoulders, pushing her back against the door, his lips but inches apart from hers. He stood there a few seconds longer breathing in the scent of Megan's perfume, soap, and shampoo all mixed in one antagonizing scent that was his own personal brand of ecstasy.

"I guess I had better get going before somebody gets to ahead of themselves and doesn't know how to finish anything." He just laughed.

Megan said shyly, "Um . . . I guess you had better be going."

Robert let himself out, smirking at her while Megan stood there watching the door close in her face. She closed her eyes whispering, "I'm just going to pretend like this never happened. Damn, I feel so stupid. Why did I just do that? Ugh damn you Robert for making me feel like this."

She stomped upstairs falling onto her bed and closing her eyes, wishing a rewind button existed in reality.

Robert drove home, dwelling in the taste of Megan, remembering the feel of his fingers dancing against her skin. His dad lay asleep on the couch as he walked through the front door. He strayed towards the fridge his hand falling automatically onto a beer. He closed and locked his basement bedroom door. Robert sat on the edge of the mattress to remove his boots and socks. He slid lazily onto the bed and slipped his shirt off over his head, allowing his bare back the privilege of the cool air from the fan. He gazed at the picture on his nightstand saying, "Maggie, what am I going to do with you?"

He laughed and placed the picture frame back onto the nightstand whispering, "I know exactly what I'm going to do with you, but I have to wait." Robert leaned his head back to rest on the wall and closed his eyes. He drank the last of his beer and placed the can gently on the table letting his thoughts overtaking his mind, drifting into a deep sleep.

Chapter Eleven

GUESS WHO

A loud knock at the front door alerted Megan, scaring her. She paused the movie, jumping over the back of the couch murmuring,

"Who in the fuck is here?"

She opened the front door slowly, heat swirling in through the crack, surrounding Megan. Robert stood there, with a smirk on his face. *Oh yeah, he's hell in person and I'm shit out of luck right now.*

"Oh it's you . . . what do you want?" Megan asked annoyed. The night air whipped at Megan as she stepped out onto the porch.

"You know what I want." murmured Robert, smirking at her. He laughed, the glow from the porch light, cascading upon him.

"Yeah . . . Don't remind me." She crossed her arms over her chest asking again, "What do you want Robert? It's late and you made me stop a damn good movie."

"I'm here to take you out on a date."

"What date . . . I never agreed to a date with you." declared Megan hoping that he would have forgotten about today's earlier events.

"Oh yes you did darling'," said Robert quickly. "Do I need to um, refresh your memory?" He stepped towards her, grinning broadly knowing that he had her now.

"No you don't have too." declared Megan. She glared at him giving in, "Fine let's go."

"Hell yea! That's what I'm talking about honey!" exclaimed Robert with a satisfied smile.

"Don't call me honey." remarked Megan. "So where are we going?"

"That is for me to know and you to find out." said Robert as he led the way to his Harley Davidson motorcycle.

"Oh okay . . . Are you sure what I'm wearing is safe?" Megan looked down at her blue jean miniskirt and boots.

"Yes and trust me because I have seen a lot worse." Robert slid on, reaching around to help Megan on. As he revved the engine up, he yelled loudly,

"Hang onto me and really tight! Okay?"

Megan nodded her head as he took off almost making Megan fall off and bust her ass. She wrapped her arms around Robert's tight, muscled waist. She snuggled her body closely against Robert's back.

"What in the hell am I doing?" whispered Megan to herself softly. He thought *I've had plenty of girls ride on my motorcycle with me, but when Megan . . . my Maggie has her body pressed against my back, it feels so right.*

He pulled into a parking lot and Megan slid off standing there gaping at the place Robert had brought her for their supposed date.

"We're going to a bar?" She glanced at Robert watching him grin happily.

"Hey it was your idea, remember?" said Robert playfully. He laughed at Megan's facial expression.

"Oh yeah," muttered Megan coldly. As they were walking to the door, Megan heard somebody hollering her name and the bad part was she recognized it immediately.

"Megan! Hey sis! What are you doing here?"

"I'm here with Robert, but just as friends."

"I don't care but hey Robert, you didn't tell me you were going to be here." shouted Joe excitedly.

"Well I am, come on let's go inside," declared Robert. The three walked in together but Joe left them standing at the entrance. Megan saw him slide in a booth with a young, but pretty girl. Robert and Megan took a booth in the corner. As they were sitting down, a waitress named Beth wandered over.

"What do ya two want?"

"A beer, a burger and . . ."

"And two order of fries with a large Pepsi," declared Megan.

"Okay. Your order will be ready in a few minutes," yelled Beth over the blasting jukebox nearby. Once the waitress left, Robert wrapped his arm around her shoulders staring at her face thinking, *Megan sure has grown up from miss little Maggie and became a hottie.*

His eyes traveled down the curve of his neckline to the top of her breasts. He made himself look away, but his gaze traveled back to her breasts, allowing himself to watch the heavy rise and fall of her chest as she breathed. Robert's fingers reached out and pulled Megan's long, silky blonde hair away from her face, draping it over her shoulder. Her hair fell down her back lying perfectly straight. He suddenly asked,

"Will you dance with me?"

"Sure, why the hell not?" answered Megan sighing bored.

He took Megan by the hand and led her out onto the dance floor. He pulled Megan close to him, liking the way her body molded against his, satisfying the feeling of the heat radiating off her body, transmitting against him. As the song ended, they walked back to the booth meeting the waitress at the table with their order. She walked away to another booth while Robert picked up his beer and took a long swig of it, feeling refreshed.

Megan coughed as Robert blew a puff of smoke towards her. She stared hard at Robert, watching him take another sip of his beer. His hand slid to her knee making Megan frown back at him. He sat smirking at her while his hand curiously slid up to the hem of her miniskirt. Robert's rough fingertips grazing her skin, Megan grabbed his hand whispering,

"That's too far," she placed his hand back to her knee saying sarcastically; "right there is just fine."

"Yeah for now," he murmured softly. He slid his hand back to the hem line of Megan's skirt and she glared back at him hatefully.

"Do you want to go home?" he asked.

"Yes!" yelled Megan over the jukebox. Robert left some bills atop the table and led Megan outside. As they approached his bike, he asked,

"Bars aren't your type of place to go for a date, are they?"

"No, not really," she whispered. Suddenly her face grew pasty white and Robert noticed.

"What's wrong?"

Megan didn't answer, just kept her gaze locked on a car across the street. The car pulled up right beside them. Megan stepped back and when Robert saw who it was, he clamped his mouth shut, staring at Megan' father, Mr. Johnson.

"Megan! What the hell are you doing here with him?" her father shouted.

"Dad, we're not dating! We are just friends."

"No the fuck it's not okay!" yelled Mr. Johnson. "Get your ass into my car!"

Megan walked into her dad's car and sat there crying. Mr. Johnson glared at Robert as he walked past him to his car. Robert thought *fuck! Yep, I'm definitely taking his ass out now. Just wait and see, but then if I do my ass is back in jail and I can't have that happen.*

Robert watched Mr. Johnson drive off with Maggie. He kicked the gravel deciding to go back in the bar to find Joe and his date. He spotted them at their booth all cuddled up. As he neared, he could see Joe's dates' boobs practically falling out of her tank top. Next he saw Joe's pants unzipped and hands all over each other.

He declared loudly, "Can I interrupt?"

Joe sat up straight and said surprised, "Hey Robert come on and slide in next to me."

"I will after you zip your jeans back up and you little cutie put your boobs away."

"Oh shit I'm sorry," murmured Joe smiling like he had been caught with his hand in the cookie jar.

"Did I offend you in any way or is it because you're gay?" Joe's girlfriend asked.

"I assure you, I'm not gay in the slightest."

"Trust me honey he's right. I can't tell you how many stories he has told me about his one night stands or how many times I've caught him."

"And my friend I have caught you just as many times too. Don't forget Joe or do I need to refresh your memory?" questioned Robert smartly.

"No I'm okay. Tammy why don't you go to the bathroom and freshen up some? We will be leaving in a few minutes."

"Be back in a few."

"Take your time," said Joe as Tammy, his girlfriend and left. Robert stole Joe's unopened beer bottle and helped himself.

Joe said, "If I remember you're still the same way."

"Not here lately Joe, I'm only chasing your sister."

"Holy shit! My sister, not again Robert, why can't you just let her memory be erased and find somebody new and actually worth your time?" proclaimed Joe honestly.

"Yes your sister and no I can't just erase her memory."

"Well good luck to ya and have fun getting around the old man."

"Oh don't worry I have already found that out." Tammy stood there asking Joe innocently,

"Are you ready to go?"

"Hell yea I'm ready to go if you are."

"Well it was nice talking to you again Joe. See you around." Robert downed the rest of the beer and slid out of the booth heading straight for the exit. He stepped out into the blanket of heat, thinking *Joe sure has not changed in the slightest. I need a new plan to get pull Megan around to my side. This is crazy . . . I'm going to end up losing my mind.*

He climbed onto his Harley and took off, spinning gravel as he pulled out onto the highway heading back home to the creek to spend some alone time.

Robert sat on the edge of the creek smirking, thinking about the good old days. The stars gazed down upon him, winking. His cell rang so he answered it.

"Hey, Robert its' Joe and I just left home. Do you want to meet me at your parent's house?"

"Sure . . . but what about Tammy?"

"I left her at home and she's asleep anyways. I told her I would be hanging out with you tonight, she doesn't mind."

"Oh okay. I'm going back home so if you want to meet me there then come on over because I need your help."

"Please tell me that it doesn't involve a certain sister of your best friend."

"Um . . . well kind of." Robert ran his hands through his hair. He sighed deeply, letting Joe know that he was in a bind and needed his help.

"I'll meet ya, Robert. We'll talk then," Robert stood up and started walking back to the road for his motorcycle. He shoved his thumbs into his front pockets of his jeans, thinking madly, *I want to touch Megan, my Maggie . . . to see her . . . to taste her. I'm obsessed with her, but I don't care.*

He questioned himself wondering if he was making the right decision by hanging onto her for so long. Robert climbed onto the porch and trotted inside easily and quietly, not really recognizing how late it was. He slipped down to the basement waiting for Joe to show up.

Megan sat on her bed thinking about Robert and her father. The plan she was bouncing around her head a wise decision. She whispered to herself,

"Yes." Megan finished writing her father and Robert a letter each. A letter to her father explaining her reasons for taking the current act she was about to take. A letter to Robert telling him to leave her family alone and that she was gone, and gone for good. She sealed the envelopes, pushing them in between her mattresses not wanting the letters to be found.

Chapter Twelve
RUNAWAY BY NIGHT

"Stand still Megan! I have only a few more curls." ordered Nana agitated. Megan stomped her foot, making her heel click harshly on the linoleum floor.

"Nana . . . It doesn't have to be perfect." murmured Megan. Bits and pieces of the sun last's rays shined down through the window casting upon Megan and her grandmother.

"Oh yes it is." Nana's gaze glared at Megan, daring her to protest further.

"Mom? Where are you?" shouted Dave loudly from the staircase.

"In Megan's bathroom!" hollered Nana. Footsteps trailing down the hard wood floor stopped slowly in the bathroom entrance.

"There's my little girl. I never thought I would ever see you so dolled up."

"Yeah well don't get used to it dad," snapped Megan.

"There I'm all done! Turn and let your father have a look at you." Megan turned slowly with her arms hanging at her sides, bored already.

"Honey, you look beautiful." said Mr. Johnson softly. He smiled truthfully at his daughter.

"Okay . . ." murmured Megan, rolling her eyes.

"Well I'm going to head on over to the Mason's house for the block party. I will meet you two there." Nana pecked Megan and her son, Dave each on the cheek. She walked past them, her dress swirling around her knees.

Dave reached for his daughter's hand pulling her into his embrace. She smiled against his big belly and wrapped her arms around his waist, always loving her father's hugs.

"Let's go and have a good time tonight." Dave walked his daughter down the stairs not realizing that Megan had plans of her own tonight once everybody was asleep.

Robert and Joe sat on a bench by the beer kegs not caring if people knew they were twenty-one or not.

"Do you even think Megan will show?"

"Knowing my father for the kind of man he is, yes he will make her will show." Joe answered knowingly. "And look who it is."

Joe pointed at the beautiful blonde standing next to their father. "There she is." Robert's gaze flickered through the crowd landing upon Megan, his Megan. Robert wiped his napkin across his face, hoping that he didn't have mustard or any ketchup o his face. He smiled at Megan hoping she would walk his way but Megan only frowned at him acting as if she didn't know who he was. She continued walking up the path into the house hoping to find Allie, but instead found Robert hurriedly walking her way. He grabbed her arm, gripping tightly saying.

"Why don't you come and sit with Joe and me for a little while?" His eyes roamed up and down her body wanting to find the nearest bedroom and lock her in there with himself.

"Please tell me why I should?" Megan questioned annoyed.

"Because I said so," he grabbed her by the arm, pulling her outside and pushing her onto the bench across from her brother, Joe. He sat down beside Megan commenting,

"Why do you always have to make things difficult?"

"And why can't you take a hint?" Megan asked angrily. Robert glared at her, reaching for his red Dixie cup. "I need a drink."

"You aren't the only one." murmured Megan. She rolled her eyes, turning her back to Robert not caring if she pissed him off. Joe glanced from Megan to Robert back to Megan, abruptly murmuring,

"I'm going to leave ya'll alone."

"Oh no you're not, you're not leaving me here alone with this man." ordered Megan sharply. "Sit down Joe." She glared at him warning Joe. He quickly sat back down feeling defeated.

"What's your problem Meg?"

"Nothing," snapped Megan.

"Fine."

"Fine." She continued to glare at the wooden fence in front of her not caring.

As darkness fell quickly down upon them, surrounding them in blackness, Megan stood by Robert hoping that she would be able to sneak away from him and soon. Her heels arched into her feet and shooting up her ankles, so Megan made an excuse.

"Robert I'm going to walk down the street to Nana's and switch my outfit and shoes. These heels are killing my feet." She looked up into his eyes, making her lips pout and soften. He gave in, falling for the charade.

"Here I will walk you home Megan."

"No, it's okay Robert, really its fine. You don't have to walk me home."

"Maybe I want to Megan?" She closed her eyes biting her tongue.

"Fine you can walk me home." He reached for her hand, tangling his fingers within her own, liking the way the soft palm of her hand lightly brushed hers.

Twinkling lights from the stars shined down upon them. Shouts and laughter from the Mason's backyard echoed in the distance. *Damn why did he have to walk me home? This is going to be harder with him around because I know for a damn fact he is going to follow me inside.*

Megan pushed the sliding door open from the back deck, just enough room for her and Robert to slide in past.

"Would you like anything to drink?" Megan questioned politely.

"Naw I'm good," Robert stood in the kitchen light, feeling slightly dazed, and a buzz from the beer.

"Well then if you would just wait in the living room for me then I will be right back because it won't take me long."

Megan turned, rushing up the last three top stairs, running to her room. Her heart pounded within her chest, pushing harder and harder. She pushed the dress over her head replacing it with worn, faded blue jeans and white tank top.

She kicked her heels off and pushed her feet into her boots not worrying because she didn't have socks on her feet or not. Megan grabbed her purse along with the two letters once for Robert and one for her dad. She walked down the stairs quietly, placing the letter for Robert on the couch. A light from the fridge door reflected off the wall, showing Megan that Robert was roaming around the refrigerator. She tip toed out the front door and into the garage.

Throwing her purse into the front seat of her car, Megan slipped her father's letter into the driver's seat of his truck. She ran to her car and climbed inside, shutting the door softly. Her fingers gripped the steering wheel, her palms drenched with sweat, not fully believing what she was about to do. Megan started the early seventeenth birthday present from her father, a Dodge Avenger and rolled out of the garage out onto the street.

Megan looked quickly behind her before she turned the lights on making sure nobody was following her, knowing only too well that she was in the clear. Letting her fingers to find the radio tuning button, she turned it to her favorite rap and R&B station.

"I'm actually doing this, oh well here goes now or never." Megan's stomach swarmed with butterflies, her heart still pounding within her chest. She pointed her car to the open highway, blasted her music knowing that she was free. *Will I ever see Robert again?*

Megan didn't care about her future anymore, only the present, only the then and the now mattered to her. Robert walked back to the living room, his eyes landing on the white envelope displaying his name in neat, black cursive handwriting. Robert reached for the envelope and ripped it open. Inside was a letter addressed to him.

He sat down heavily on the couch, unfolding the papers to read the letter. His eyes sucked in every word, every detail and only after finishing the letter did he yell out in fury. Robert crumpled the letter within his fist, tossing it onto the table before him.

Robert stood up, taking the stairs two at a time. As he stood before Megan's bedroom door, he kicked it open, only to find her room black and empty. He turned and ran outside into the dark, feeling a cool breeze attack his body and rush his mind.

"Megan, I promise to hunt you down. I promise to make your family pay and suffer. I promise to make you pay and hurt and feel pain!" shouted Robert into the empty night.

Chapter Thirteen
BREAKFEST SHOWDOWN

"It sure is a fine morning, ain't it Megan?" declared Uncle Clint Matthews cheerfully.

"Oh yes it sure is," answered Megan gravely, as they sat down at the kitchen table to eat breakfast. Clint whipped out his newspaper from his back pocket, flipping to the front page, lazily reading the current events that had happened in Magnum, Oklahoma. She thought *I want to go back to Kentucky and visit Abby's grave site. I miss her so much and I really need her more than anything in my life right now.*

"You look tired Meg, honey. How late did you and Shannon stay out last night with the guys?" asked Aunt Annie. She stood around for a couple of seconds, gazing into Megan's eyes, knowing why she was so upset and it was not from lack of sleep either. "Later you and I are going to sit down, have a nice glass of sweet tea, and talk. Okay?"

"Yes ma'am." Megan looked up into her aunt's loving, bronze face and smiled. "I guess you could stay that I got in about one or two this mornin'." Her uncle stared blankly at her over his cup of coffee and Megan continued, "Don't worry though I'll still get my chores and work done around here." As she finished her sentence, two little boys came running down the stairs, shouting happily.

"Hey, my early birds are ya'll hungry?" cooed Annie softly.

"Yes momma, we hungry." exclaimed Jimmy.

Megan opened her mouth to correct his grammar, but Clint shot a glare that told her, don't worry about it. So she left it alone and went back to eating. Annie fixed the boys' plates and helped them up to the table. Millie and Shannon came down the stairs into the kitchen still in their pajamas, hair rumpled and mascara smeared.

Clint asked harshly, "Girls? Why aren't ya'll dressed yet? You were supposed to be up at six-thirty helping your brother Chad and Megan feed the livestock." He shot them a disapproved look that made the girls insides knot and twist in fear. Shannon tried her excuse first.

"Sorry dad but I was tired from getting in late last night . . . actually early this morning." Megan sipped her coffee, minding her own business with her eyes cast down on the kitchen table. She thought *Shannon's done it now.* She couldn't hide her smirk though.

Shannon caught it and whipped around saying, "What are you smirking about? Huh? What's so funny?"

"Your face," Megan sat there, not taking her eyes off the table replying sarcastically.

"Bitch. I will come across this table and wipe that silly smirk off your face." Megan jolted up shaking the table, declaring,

"Shannon, please don't start this shit again. Look just because your boyfriend preferred my company better than yours then it's your lost. I can't help you're always jealous of me."

"What did you just say?" Shannon flashed daggers at Megan. She stood her ground saying,

"If you would just pull your head out of your own ass you would've been able to tell that it was his identical twin, Devin not your boyfriend, Danny. Plus, if you were going to do something then you would have already done it. Oh, but wait there's more, your boyfriend was actually out with Courtney Davis."

"What . . . what do you mean? No, Danny wouldn't do something like that to me."

"You want to try that answer again? He's been cheating on you for the last three months with her. He knows he can get it from her and not from you so . . . hell I wouldn't blame him. The way you're always walking around here like your Ms. High and Mighty. Did you put the tampon in wrong this morning, just thought I'd ask."

Megan stood there knowing that she had won this battle with her cousin. Shannon stood quiet, tears dribbling from the corners of her eyes, whimpering before taking off upstairs to dwell. Megan nodded her head in approval and turned to answer her aunt and uncle's blank faces. Clint stared at her amazed.

"It's about damn time that somebody said something to her. I hope you finally put her in her place where she belongs. She needed it and badly. Thank you Megan, you are my hero!"

Annie smiled at her softly saying, "Thank you Megan." She turned back to the dirty dishes in the sink.

Uncle Clint asked, "Now Mille, what about you? What is your excuse or would you rather have a showdown with Megan this morning?"

"Um . . . no I think I'll pass." She backed away, before shooting off upstairs to check on Shannon. Nobody seemed to notice Chad standing in the doorway with a calf in his arms until it started to bawl. Everybody turned their attention to Chad and their unexpected guest.

Clint asked, "What's wrong son?"

"The calf's broken her leg. I found her down in the creek, back in between some boulders as I making my morning rounds."

"Okay well put the calf in the bed of my truck. I'll have Shannon and Millie tag along with me, so you can stay here to finish that fence."

"Okay dad," Chad answered plainly, kicking the door softly to enter the sizzling heat once again.

"Annie, will you go tell the girls to get dressed? I want them to go with me to the vet clinic. Tell both the girls to wear something decent this time." Annie left the kitchen, murmuring to herself.

Clint turned, stepping outside to join his son at the barn to help get hay for bedding in the truck. Megan met Chad and Clint at the truck watching Shannon and Millie walk their way.

"Hey, Shannon how are you feeling this morning?"

"Shut the fuck up!" shouted Shannon threw gritted teeth. She climbed in the front seat of the truck without saying another word. Millie didn't even look at Megan. She just climbed into the backseat slamming the door shut.

As Clint started the truck and rolled the windows down, Megan shouted at Shannon, "I hope you don't run into Courtney Davis while in town."

Chad stared back and forth between his sister and cousin wondering what in the hell did he miss this morning. He scratched the bill of his camouflage hat on his head and continued to stand there looking confused.

"Okay, did I miss somethin' this mornin' that I'm supposed to know about?"

"I guess you could say that." Megan bit down on her bottom lip, stopping herself from laughing.

"Well what in the hell was it? Did something happen last night?"

"Yeah, well kind of."

"Okay, woman either you tell me what it was or I'm just going to flat out tackle your ass!" He stopped walking, planting his feet firmly, demanding an answer.

"Um . . . It was a great victory, I will tell you that."

"That's it!" Chad grabbed Megan around her knees, throwing her over his shoulder, and spinning around a couple of times. She hollered, laughing harder and harder. "Chad! Put me down."

He planted her back on her feet softly saying, "Now tell me."

"I thought you said that you were going to tackle me?"

"I will if you don't tell me. Now, spill the beans." He stared at her trying not to grin, knowing that Megan knew he was only kidding.

She murmured, "Fine I will tell you. You'll hear about it anyways. Okay, well you know how Shannon and I went to the usual hangout spot with the guys. Well her boyfriend wasn't there, but his twin Devin was. I was talking to him, goofing off and hanging out with him for most of the night and early morning. Shannon thought that it was her boyfriend, thinking that I was hitting on him and she threw this huge fight. I commented to her about this morning, and well I knew the whole night where her man was."

"Let me guess Megan, he was with Courtney Davis?"

"How the hell did you know so quickly?"

"I didn't; I just guessed. Shannon mentioned something about her to me . . . I don't remember what the hell it was about so anyways continue."

"It was glorious. You just had to be there this morning."

"Man I wish I had stayed home and gone out later to check on the herd." He kicked his foot at the ground, stirring up dust as he walked beside Megan. He thought *damn it I wish I had been there. I would have loved to have seen Megan put Shannon in her place.*

"Hey do you want to go horse riding with me?"

"Sure let's go. It's been awhile since you and I spent any time together," answered Megan. "Plus there's not really anything much we have to do, right? Except finish putting the new fence up, but that doesn't take too long for us." She jogged after Chad to keep up with him and his long strides as they entered the horse stables.

She unlatched the door and stepped into Sunshine's stall, rubbing up and down her face. Chad led Moonshine out of his stall into the alley way of the barn. He went into the tack room and grabbed his saddle, bridle, and saddle bags. He walked to Moonshine, slid all of his equipment onto his horse shouting,

"Hey Meg, are you ready?"

"Hell yes I am! Let's ride!"

"Sounds damn good to me," Chad mounted Moonshine, settling into the saddle, and rearranging the veins evenly. Meg sat there patiently waiting for Chad to get settled.

He whipped around, asking, "Ready?"

"Hell yeah, I was born ready!" Chad raised his head and laughed heartedly at Megan's comment. Chad and Megan dug their spurs into the side of their horses gently, persuading them to walk. They rode out of the barn, receiving a gentle breeze. They traveled slowly down the driveway first then decided to cut left and head down the old, worn dirt trail to the back pastures. As they neared the edge of the driveway, Megan and Chad noticed a black, Harley Davidson coming their way. They reined up their horses, waiting for the man on the bike to stop.

Chad asked friendly, "May I help you?"

"Um . . . yeah I'm looking for my girl whom I used to date bout a year ago."

"What's her name and I might know her. Did she move here just recently?"

"No actually she moved here 'bout a year ago."

"Then I don't know who she is, because the only girl that moved here 'bout a year ago was my cousin . . . unless?" Chad turned to Megan and flashed his gaze back to the stranger sitting on the motorcycle.

"Oh yes you know her, you know her very well. Hello Megan, my dear."

"Me . . ." Megan flipped her gaze from Chad to the man wondering just who in the hell he was. *Holy shit! It's fucking Robert. Damn it, how in the hell did he find me?* "Robert?"

"Hello love," Robert pulled his aviators off and turned to Megan, spreading a smirk. He thought *this is going to be fun.* He sat amazed at how much Megan had changed, had grown up.

Megan sat atop Sunshine, observing Robert, seeing what had changed and what hadn't. *I've got to leave because I can't let him see my pain. I have to be strong and not give into my emotions. I'm grown up and I'm different, I'm not that same young, silly teenager anymore and I'm going to make him see that.*

Chapter Fourteen
HE'S BACK

Megan jerked on her horse's reins, pulling her to the right and running back to the stables. She jumped off Sunshine and led her into the corral next to the horse barn. She ran up the porch steps and inside. When she saw Robert stop in front of the house and get off his motorcycle, Megan stepped out onto the porch, planting her feet firmly, standing her ground.

Robert said eagerly, "Hey Megan, how have ya been?"

"Great since you haven't been around and don't you hey Megan me. How in the hell did you find me? You're not supposed to be here!" yelled Megan.

"First, what am I doing here? I think you know exactly why I'm here. Second, I had Joe tell me." She stood there, thoughts racing through her head.

"Joe? Naw he wouldn't have told you that," she declared firmly.

Robert started her way, jogging up the porch steps. He stood but a few inches away from her. She could smell his scent, his cologne. His curly black hair was damp from the Oklahoma heat so early in the morning. She could see a few droplets of sweat sliding down his neck hiding itself beneath his red, cut off sleeveless shirt. Megan let her gaze roam to its muscles, trying hard not to stare but it became obvious because Robert flexed his muscles and she tore her gaze away, letting her eyes settle back onto his face. She stared into his brown, creamy chocolate eyes, feeling like she disappeared into time, to never come back.

He stepped to her, filling the empty gap between them, running his fingertips up and down the lengths of her arms. Cold chills and goose bumps came and went as Robert stood entranced in the moment, never wanting it to end. He leaned his head in toward her ear, breathing hotly on her cheek, her ear, and her neck.

Chad came up behind Robert, standing six foot five, same height as Robert. He asked him,

"Are you Robert Anderson?"

"Why yes I am, sad to say," murmured Robert bitterly. He closed his eyes thinking *dude you ruined the moment.* Megan raised her eyes, settling them back on Robert, wishing that he would just leave and leave for good.

"You're not supposed to be here mister."

Robert straightened up to full height whispering, "Ya think I don't already know that. Can't a man have a little privacy around here anymore?"

Chad dared him to say anything else. "So why are you here?" asked Chad edging Robert on.

"I'm here for Megan, so if you don't mind we have some very important, unfinished business to attend to, if you know what I mean." He wrapped a fist around Megan's upper arm, demanding, "Come on Megan let's go back to my place where we can be who we want to be and have privacy."

She stood her ground firmly, not moving her feet knowing exactly what Robert was getting at.

"Look mister, I mind you being here and I'm gona have to ask you to leave sir. Please?" asked Chad nicely. "I'm askin' ya kindly. What do ya say?"

Robert released her arm answering, "Sure, I'll go but this isn't the last time you will see me around here." He turned, walking in long strides to his motorcycle. He straddled his bike, driving off quickly, leaving a long, thick trail of dust.

She collapsed onto the white, painted porch, Chad sitting heavily down beside her. He ran his hands through his hair asking lazily,

"What are ya going to do now, cuz?"

Megan raised her head up and gazed out at the wide open space. *I don't see how he tracked me down. If Joe did really tell him I'm going to beat the shit out of him.*

"I don't know what I'm going to do Chad because the one place that I thought I had found solitude and closure, the rug gets ripped out from beneath my feet." She sighed deeply continuing, "The way I see it I have only two options. One, stick it out or leave and move away. But I know that if I do leave and move, he'll just follow me. If I stick it out, there will be hell to pay for you and your family. I don't want anybody to get hurt."

Chad wrapped an arm around Megan's shoulder. *If I see that guy again he's going to be six feet under.*

"Don't worry Meg. We're here for you and I'm defiantly here for you."

"Okay," whispered Megan not convinced. She stared at Chad and couldn't help herself but smile. Chad flashed that smile that always won the heart of the ladies. He stood up and picked Megan up off the steps pushing her inside the house. Chad handed her a water bottle while he said,

"Now you know that I have to call dad and tell him. You know that, don't you?"

"Yeah, I guess I always figured that he'd come for me sooner or later." She shrugged her shoulders.

Chad stood up and walked out onto the back deck. She stared down at the counter, exhaling deeply. *Why, can't the man ever give up for once? Come on there are plenty of hot, tall blondes out in this world. Why can't the man take no for an answer?*

Robert looked left then right before pulling into a café. As he walked in, the noticed a truck with the Matthews brand on the side. He smiled to himself, ready to put his plan into action.

"Hello, Clint here?"

Dave warned us about? Well he came by the house today wanting to see Megan."

"Is that prick still there?" Clint growled angrily at Chad.

"No sir, so don't worry,"

"Hell, there's no point in telling me that I'm going to worry. I love Megan like a daughter. Okay well I'm on my way home. Tell Megan not to worry son."

"Yes sir," replied Chad hurriedly as he hung up. He walked back inside talking to Megan. "Uncle's on his way home." Megan shook her head in reply. *Great, just great now everything is going to happen all over again, just like back in Georgia. I don't want this to be happening, it can't be.* She laid her head on the cool, black marble counter.

Robert drank his coke and ate his club sandwich in silence and alone. He left some bills on the counter and walked out. He stood outside the café inhaling the freshness of the country air, *beats the city,* thought Robert. He walked to his motorcycled and drove away to his apartment his thoughts consumed of Megan and nothing else.

A truck pulled up in front of the house a few minutes later, stirring dust, and throwing gravel as it was into park. Chad stood on the porch thinking *who in the hell is this fool? Oh never mind it's just the twins.* The boys stepped down out of their truck and swaggered over to Chad. Megan heard voices outside the kitchen. She whispered her voice full of malice.

"If that's Robert I'm going to knock his ass out." She kicked the screen door open, stomping out onto the deck shouting, "Robert if . . ." She stopped dead in her tracks once she saw the twins standing there with goofy grins staring back at her. "Hey! What are you two doing here?"

Megan walked to Devin allowing him to pick her up in a big bear hug, swinging her around a few times. He passed her into Danny's waiting arms, following suit of his brother. Danny released Megan and stood there, her face flushed.

"So Danny where were you last night?"

"I was at home sick," He faked a cough and commented, "I'm pulling your leg. I was busy, actually very busy last night."

"Oh yeah, you were busy from what I've heard. You've been really busy." She patted Danny on the cheek and winked at him. Devin put his hand over his mouth trying to hide his smile. Chad looked over and saw his dad pulling up in the driveway. Shannon shot out of the truck, stomping over to Danny. She planted her feet firmly in the dust, standing in front of him. She pulled her fist back, slapping him across the left cheek.

Shannon turned, ready to walk away when Danny yelled, "Bitch! What the fuck was that for?"

"You know perfectly damn well why I slapped you. How dare you show your two-timing face here!"

"What are you talking about?" Danny flashed his gaze at Megan, Chad, Devin as they took a few steps out of line of fire. He returned his attention back to Shannon.

Devin whispered softly, "This is going to be good. Hey, Chad do ya'll have any popcorn in the house?"

"I think so . . . Why? Do you think we're going to need some?" asked Chad loudly not caring if he was overheard or not.

"For this showdown . . . oh yeah you betcha." Megan snickered and looked at Devin, trying so hard not to laugh. She heard Shannon ask,

"So what the hell is this shit about that I'm hearing about you and that county whore Courtney Davis?" Danny snapped his mouth shut and his ears turned beet red. *Well it looks like he's been caught with his hand down the wrong cookie jar or just caught with his zipper down with the wrong girl.*

"Aren't you going to answer me?" Shannon waited, while seconds ticked by before continuing. "No, you're not because its true isn't it?"

Shannon's eyes brimmed with tears while mascara and eyeliner smeared her eyes and cheeks. She stared at Danny dumbfounded and shouted, "It's over Danny! Don't come around here ever again!" That being the final word said, she stomped off, flinging the screen door open and running inside. Danny turned to Devin, gave him a high five and said,

"Thank you so much Megan, sweet innocent Megan! Why don't you hook up with my little brother here?" He flashed a huge grin, stretching from ear to ear.

"Little brother, huh? Danny you're only two minutes older me, lay off!"

"Fine." Danny turned back to Megan and opened her hand palm up saying sweetly,

"Money, please?"

"Oh yeah that is right, ain't it? Here ya go my lady." answered Danny as he whipped out his wallet, laying a fifty dollar bill on her palm as Megan's fingers wrapped around the green paper, sliding her payment into her back packet.

Danny said, "Bro, you ready to head out?"

"No not really," Devin threw a glance at Megan saying, "But we have to leave don't we?"

"I'm sorry but you know good and well that if we don't, dad will chew our asses out, again." Danny replied angrily. He turned to Devin and said, "Let's go. You can always come back over after work, you got Megan's number. Call her up and take sweet little thing Megan out tonight, but if you do, you are picking her up in your own truck this time mister."

"Yeah . . . you're right," Devin replied, smiling at Megan. Danny slung his arm over his twin's shoulder whispering loud enough for Megan to hear though.

"You never know you might get lucky."

"Danny Lee Scotts!" Megan reached over to hit him in the face, but missed hitting his ear instead. He ran off to his pickup truck, jumped inside, and locked the doors. Danny rolled the window up so Megan couldn't reach him, but left a fraction down yelling,

"Ha-ha! What are you going to do now missy? You can't touch me . . . hah!"

"Oh you just wait I'll get your ass. Don't you worry about that." She stuck out her tongue as she walked off towards Chad and Devin, as they burst out laughing.

Devin stared at Megan saying softly, "Well I guess I had better go."

"I'll call ya tonight and we'll go out and have some fun."

"Better not be too much fun or I'm going to be whipping me some ass." declared Chad warningly.

"Oh, Chad leave the guy alone . . ."

"I wasn't talking about him, I was talking about you. If I hear one little piece of scrap of information I'm kicking your ass. Then I'm coming for yours bro." replied Chad cautioning Megan.

"You don't have to worry about me."

"Sure." commented Chad. Devin smiled at Megan's loving, angelic face and thought *I love her and I'm going to tell her tonight. I want us to officially be declared and known as a couple from now on.*

"I'm only messing with ya." Chad grinned at Devin and said,

"Well I'm going to get back to work now. Come on Meg, you'll get to see him late." Chad started towards the barn and Megan watched him walk off. She turned her attention back to Devin. He said calmly, "I'll call ya as soon as I get off from work. We will talk 'bout the details later."

"Sounds good, Devin." She stepped up on tip-toes trying to reach his height, all six foot four of him. He picked her up off her feet easily as if she were a baby doll. He squeezed her gently, pecking her on the cheek. Devin turned, heading for the truck. He waved at Megan and Danny stuck his tongue out at her. She flicked her middle finger at him and started towards the barn to hunt Chad down.

Chapter Fifteen
MAN CAVE STYLE

"So you're telling me that Robert was here?" Clint shouted outraged.

"Yes, sir." answered Chad. Megan sat in silence watching, her eyes following her uncle's every movement. He flashed his eyes coldly at Megan, back to his son, before throwing the screen door wide open and walking off to his office.

Megan leaned back into the swing, pulling her blue jean shorts down. The indigo, spacious star, speckled sky stared down at her. She whispered, "He has no reason to be here. I don't understand why he had to show up and drag the past back the present all over again."

A truck approached the porch, flashing their headlights. Megan jumped off the swing and ran for Devin's truck. As she climbed in, Devin sang,

"Hey there good lookin' whatcha got cookin' for me?" She smiled her sexiest smile at him as he whispered, "come here darlin'."

She slid over next to him, while Devin put the truck in reverse. He draped an arm over her shoulders with his other hand on the wheel. Megan asked curiously,

"Where are we going?"

"You'll see, trust me. It made me think of something you said a couple of weeks ago?"

"Like what?" She raised her eyebrow in curiosity thinking *What is this crazy country boy up to now?*

"You'll see, just be patient okay?" Megan flashed him a dazzling white smile, making his heart jump.

The cool, night breeze slithered lightly through the blanket of heat surrounding Megan as she tip-toed up the stairs past her aunt and uncle's bedroom door. She kicked her boots off and collapsed on her bed staring out her window at the moon while it hung fully developed and shining clearly down upon her.

"Robert needs to leave me alone and get a new hobby. It's almost as if he's become obsessive over me." Thoughts of tonight swam throughout Megan's head. *Spending time with Devin, just lying there talking about our lives, dreams, and wants out of life was simple, but relaxing.*

"Hey there hot stuff!" She whipped her head around and laughed. Chad stood there in a baby pink striped thong pulled over his boxers and a matching bra over his chest, a cowboy hat and slip on boots. His socks practically pulled up to his knees and aviators flashing at Megan. He twirled a pair of black briefs on his hand that had Devin's name written all over in big, bold hot pink letters.

Devin appeared behind Chad, laughing and staring at Megan as she walked over to them. She asked,

"Is that my thong . . . and matching bra?"

"Why yes it is darlin'." Chad answered huskily.

He laughed and looked at Devin, wiping tears away from his eyes and trying to catch his breath. Devin said,

"Hey babe . . . sorry but we've had this planned for several hours and we were ready to put it to the test. You see we got this whole talent show thing coming up at work this week sometime."

"That's okay," she stared at them in amazement and couldn't help, but laugh. She leaned against the door frame shaking her head at them. Megan smirked, still trying to wrap her brain around the concept at hand that was happening to her at two-thirty in the morning. Devin stopped laughing, and asked,

"Do you think I could stay the night?" Chad stared at him, saying.

"I don't care . . . Hey, why don't you call your brother and see if he wants to stay also? We will have guy night! Party! Party!" The guys chanted together.

"Here, call Danny because I'm going to spend some time with your cousin then." Devin stepped towards her, placing his hands on her hips, standing there still just staring into her eyes, watching them sparkle. *Megan's my jewel, my diamond.*

She stepped back, Devin never letting go of her waist. They kept walking back until she came in contact with the bed behind her. He laid down on the bed beside Megan, whispering.

"Do you think your aunt and uncle would get mad if I sleep with you in your bed?"

"Probably not because Clint let Danny and Shannon sleep to get her all the time when he came to stay over. Why?" She stared into his eyes murmuring, "Nothing is going to happen."

"I know that," Devin said softly. He kissed her on the forehead and she got up walking to her dresser grabbing a tank top and cotton shorts. Closing the bathroom door behind her to change, Chad appeared with a thirty pack of Coors Light beer still wearing the sexy outfit. He walked in saying,

"Do you want a beer? Danny will be here in about ten, fifteen minutes?"

"Where is he coming from?" Devin questioned as he sat up reaching for a beer. "Oh wait let me guess, Courtney Davis?"

"You betcha but hey where's Megan?"

"She went to the bathroom to change. Um . . . this is kind of weird asking you this, but would it be a problem if I sleep here tonight, I mean with Meg?" Chad stood there shrugging his shoulders.

He said, "I don't care but if I hear anything about any hanky panky you're both in trouble."

"Chad? Seriously . . . I'm your best friend next to my twin, but really?"

"I'm kidding . . . I trust you man." Chad walked over to Devin, giving him a hug.

"This is awkward." Megan exclaimed standing there watching her cousin and Devin.

"Hey we're men we can hug if we want too and show some affection."

"If you say so boys, but next time warn me." She flipped her light off and climbed in bed, pulling the light purple sheet up over her body, asking, "So what's the game plan?"

"Well Danny . . ."

"Party!" Pounded a voice out of the darkness hollering loudly.

"Is here," Megan said completing Devin's sentence. "If he brought his fuck buddy Courtney Davis, don't you guys dare dump her off on me, do you guys hear me?"

"She didn't come she doesn't even know that Danny's here, she was in the shower while he grabbed his clothes and lit out of her bedroom, butt ass naked climbing into his truck." Danny ran thundering up the stairs, appearing behind the boys wearing nothing more than boxers, boots and a cowboy hat shouting,

"Come on guys, its' party time. Why are we all standing out in the open?" He turned to look at Chad saying, "Nice get up man."

"Hey thanks . . . Ya'll ready to head down to the man cave?"

"Hell yeah!" Danny and Chad took of the man cave chanting, "Party! Party!"

"Megan said softly, "Go join the guys, I know you do so go have some fun."

"Are ya sure baby?"

"Yes."

"I'll be back up in a few hours to join you in bed. Ya know I was thinking, we have been dating for almost two years and I still can't believe that nobody has found out that we have been together all this time ya know honey?" Devin exclaimed anxiously.

"I know, but that happens when we just play it off as friends in front of family and friends." replied Megan. He sat down beside Megan, kissing her up and down her arm lightly. Danny burst in, hitting his twin on the butt with an empty, beer can.

He hollered, "Bro come on! Are you going to party with us or not?" Devin flipped his middle finger to his twin and said,

"Buzz off can't ya see I'm a little busy?" That didn't affect Danny in the slightest because he took a running start, jumping onto Devin, crushing him. His face was pressed next to Megan's and she said,

"Hi. Can I help you?"

"Yeah tell your boyfriend to get his ass down to the man cave and party with us."

He winked at her, flushing her, his dazzling white, even smile. She said,

"I will don't worry."

"Danny! You're crushing me! Get off!" Danny jumped up and pulled Devin off the bed. He said,

"Come on, let's go!"

"All right, well I'm going to have a few with the boys and will be back soon," whispered Devin.

"Okay," Megan smiled at him, her insides swarming with butterflies. Devin bent over, kissing her on the cheek, following his twin out the door.

Robert flicked his cigarette, the ashes floating in the night air, falling slowly to the dry, dust covered ground. His eyes roaming over the land beneath the dark sky, stars as they winked back at him.

"Oh Maggie, Maggie . . . What am I going to do with you?" He laughed deep in his throat, loving the ideas, swimming through his head of his dear Megan. A phone rang, loudly, echoing in the blackness.

"Hello?"

Megan lay cuddled within her bed asleep, no longer able to resist the temptation of sleep that was crouching upon her. Devin sat on the edge, watching Megan, marveling over how beautiful she looked, lying bundled in the covers sleeping in sweet serenity. He pulled back the covers allowing him to curl up next to his love. He reached for Megan, pulling her body next to his. She stirred slightly, whispering words Devin couldn't understand. He was amazed at how well their bodies molded together, as one.

Thoughts of Megan and him making love slithered throughout his mind. He wondered at how their bodies would mold, fit as one as their limbs lay tangled within each other. Devin smiled, waiting for the day they would take that next step, but he knew that he could wait and that he would. He curled up closer to Megan, resting his head near hers, inhaling her flowery shampoo. Devin felt relaxed and happy knowing that he was laying there holding the girl he loved deeply and uncontrollably since the first day he laid eyes upon her, two years ago.

A camera lens zoomed in on Megan and the body sleeping next to her.

"Shit! The boss is going to have a field day when he hears about this."
He sat there wondering what in the hell he needed to do, but decided it'd
be best to call the boss and ask him for further directions.

"Hello?" Robert murmured softly.

"Hey, you're never going to believe this but Megan has a guy in bed
with her."

"What!" Robert bolted up not believing what he was hearing.

"Yes."

"You mean sleeping or . . ." He couldn't bring himself to say the
words.

"Only sleeping . . . What do you want me to do?"

"I want you to make his ass disappear and as soon as possible." Robert
whispered something in nothing but complete curse words making his
accomplice hesitate before speaking.

"Are you sure?"

"Fuck yes I'm sure! Damn that is why I hired you."

"Don't get pissy with me boss . . . I can walk anytime and you know
that! But you know deep down that you need me." Robert clamped his
mouth shut knowing that his friend was right. "It will cost you extra."

"Deal."

His boss ended the conversation, thinking about what all he needed
to get ready for action. Robert sat on the hood of his car thinking to
himself, *so miss little Maggie has a boyfriend does she? That bitch! How dare
she? Because that means she doesn't love me.*

A voice shouted mentally deep within Robert back at him, *what the
fuck makes you so sure that she loved you before all of this shit happened?*
Robert screamed back, but aloud,

"She's mine! Maggie is mine!"

Sunday morning approached slowly. The Matthews Family usually
attending church together as a family, but Clint decided to let Chad and
Megan stay home for this one time only. Of course he knew the Scotts'
twins showing up at around one or two in the morning wanting to have
guy night. Clint murmured,

"What am I going to do with them boys?"

Clint stepped out into the heart, his body almost immediately
drenched in sweat. Megan sat up, stretching to find Devin sleeping next

to her. His head lay on her side of the mattress while his hand flopped around on the sheets seeking her body.

She leaned over, pushing the pillow to the floor of Devin's face and kissing him softly on the forehead. Megan looked once more at Devin, smiled at his sleeping, sexy body before descending down the stairs to the kitchen expecting to find the guys sitting there waiting and demanding breakfast. Instead, Megan only found the kitchen empty of bodies. She reached for the coffee pot, pouring herself a cup of coffee. She approached the screen door, a hot breeze meeting her.

Chad stood in the kitchen reaching for the coffee pot. He murmured,

"Yep that hit the spot."

Megan turned and said a little too cheerfully, "Good morning."

"Good morning to you too but what's for breakfast?"

"Pancakes and sausage coming right up," Megan answered, smiling brightly at her cousin.

"Ahh hell yeah! Megan's famous pancakes," declared Danny.

"Ha-ha . . . they aren't that famous."

"Well darlin' they are with me." Danny planted a kiss on Meg's cheek as Devin walked in.

"Good morning boys," He walked over to Megan and slipped his arms around her slender waist, kissing her fully on the lips.

"Ready for breakfast?"

"Hell yes!" shouted Danny.

Chapter Sixteen
LET THE DAY BEGIN

Megan and Chad walked outside into the heat watching the twins leave for their farm. They waved at Danny and Devin hollering,

"Bye!" Megan stood watching, turning her attention to Chad.

He asked, "So talk to me missy, what did you and Devin do last night on ya'lls date?"

"Well he came and picked me up around eleven, driving us to an abandoned hay field. We lay on the hood of his truck watching the moon and the stars. We played a game, whoever counted the most shooting stars, won a kiss from the loser. It was a fun but we also talked about life in general. How we want to get married, have kids, and what our goals are later in life."

"That's nice, but why are you two thinking about getting married when you all have only been dating for what like a day?"

"Um . . . actually we've been dating undercover for almost two years now since I moved here."

"Are you fucking serious?"

"Yes I am . . . we didn't want people knowing that we were dating."

"It all makes sense about everything." Chad walked back inside, sitting down at the kitchen table, finishing his coffee, and shaking his head in bewilderment.

Stepping out of her private bathroom, she walked over to her laptop to sign onto her Facebook webpage. Megan ran her long, skinny callused fingers through her curls murmuring,

"I hope Mimi has emailed me back because I haven't heard any new s about her surgery yet and I hope everything went okay." Flipping through her emails, she saw a message from somebody saying they're "The Watcher". She read out loud,

"Dear Megan, you made a mistake last night. I saw what you did because now you're going to pay for this Maggie, dearest. You're in so much trouble for sleeping with Devin. You better watch yourself because things are going to get intense. So if you enjoy living, you'd better not make anymore stupid mistakes."

Megan leaned back from the laptop screen and glared, knowing only one person ever called her Maggie anymore and that was Robert. She logged off completely, but not before saving the message. She stood up almost knocking the chair to the ground hearing Chad's voice.

"Megan!" She jogged out onto the porch and saw Chad sitting on the swing. He smiled at her, waving Megan over to join him. "Hey what are you doing?"

"Nothing, really I just grabbed a quick shower and checked my email . . . why?"

"Has Mimi emailed you back?"

"No." replied Megan. She inclined her head to the side, observing his face and wondering what he was thinking.

Chad flipped his hat off his head and placed it on his knee, "It's starting to cool down now. The sky is darkening I bet it rains."

"I hope it rains," She gazed at the flower pot sitting by the screen door and lost herself in her thoughts. Megan heard a voice from far off and Chad asked again,

"Meg? Hello . . . Are you there?"

"What? Oh yeah sorry I'm here I just got lost in la la land. Now what did you ask?"

"Are you okay?" He raised his eyes in curiosity.

"Yeah, I'm fine Chad. I think I'm going to go lay down for a bit though."

"Okay you do that and holler at me if you need anything."

Megan stood up and walked back inside, heading for her room. As she gazed deeply at the bluish-black angry clouds, she drifted off.

Thunder roared outside Robert's window of his living room.

"I wonder what Megan is doing? Oh never mind, I see what she's doing." He stood up and walked into the kitchen, making himself a sandwich. Robert brought it into the living room and sat down on his black, leather couch flipping the station to HBO, catching the beginning of one of his favorite movies, Risky Business with Tom Cruise.

Chapter Seventeen

WATCH YOUR STEP

Robert sat low in his car across the street, watching Megan and her aunt putting their groceries away in Meg's truck. He smiled to himself thinking *she doesn't even know that I'm over here.* He laughed to himself and pulled out his camera from inside his shirt pocket, snapping a few pictures, before driving away down the street.

Megan stared at the car driving past her and noticed that the car seemed really familiar. She turned back to the groceries shaking her head, thinking *you're just being paranoid.* Having packed all the bags in the backend of the pickup truck, they pulled out of Old Ed's Grocery Store. Megan exclaimed,

"It's dry out here again today, except the wind. Look at the clouds, they're still here but nothing has happened yet. That's the only thing that I miss about Kentucky and it's the weather because it was never too hot or too cold."

"I know we haven't had any rain for over the last three weeks. The weather forecast says that it's supposed to rain today and all the way through into next week."

"Tell me about it." Megan slowed down as the car in front of her pulled off onto the upcoming road. She put her left hand out the window, leaning it against the door and cranked her radio up as she drove past her friend, Mimi's house. She asked,

"Have you spoken to Mimi's parents? I haven't heard a single word from her."

"Yes, actually I did. Her mom was pumping gas two days ago and I asked her about Mimi and she said that she in recovery right now from her surgery."

"You know I'm not trying to be a complete bitch, ya know what happened to her, was her own fault. If she hadn't been drinking, then she wouldn't have had to have surgery ya know? And her finance would still be alive."

"I know honey but there isn't anything that we can do about it, now is there? Even us talking about it, isn't going to make things any better." Annie said softly. She glanced at her niece saying, "Well I hope that this accident has proven to some older teens that they need to be careful about drinking alcohol and they need to set an example for the younger teens."

Aunt Annie pushed some stray hairs behind Megan's ear. "You'd better turn that radio down before your uncle gets mad at us."

"Okay," exclaimed Megan. Her aunt rolled down the passenger side window and smiled, gazing over at Megan. She returned the smile back at her. As they pulled into the driveway, her aunt's German Shephard came running to greet them.

"Rosie!" She barked at them as they followed her up the drive, parking the truck next to her son's. Annie and Megan got out, walking to the bed of the truck. They carried the groceries into the house as her uncle walked by accompanied with Chad and Devin both smiling at her. Devin's heart melted when she saw him standing there, he wrapped his arms comfortably around her, murmuring in her ear.

"I missed you." He released her, stepped back, and smiled down at her. He pressed his lips to hers and whispered, "I love you Megan." Clint walked over to them and said,

"Afternoon, Meg. Having a nice day?"

"I am now." She laughed, asking. "Devin what are you doing here? I thought you said that you had to work with your dad at the feed mill today."

"I did, but he got sick so he said Danny and me could have the day off. I called Chad asking where you were and Clint invited me over. I'm helping them work in the vegetable garden."

"Well I'm glad you came over."

"I'm glad I came over."

Clint asked, "Did you all run into Robert any?"

"No uncle, we sure didn't."

"Good. Now kids be good because Annie and I are going to go take our afternoon nap." Annie put the rest of the groceries up and then followed her husband down the hall to their large master bedroom.

Chad asked, "If they pop out with anymore kids, I'm moving out."

"Well if they do and you move out, I'll gladly take your room over for you." Devin commented humorously.

Chad glared at him saying, "I'm fine but thanks. I'll catch up with ya'll later. I'm going to hop in the shower because Mattie is back in town from college so I'm going over to her house for supper tonight. I'll be home tomorrow or Tuesday sometime. I haven't decided when I'm coming back home yet because she doesn't have school until the end of this week."

"Stay at Mattie's as long as you want Chad." said Megan, smiling at her cousin. "Before you head out, where are Millie and Shannon?"

"We put them to work today." Chad smiled evilly, laughing harshly.

"Okay." Megan grabbed Devin's hand, leading him upstairs to her bedroom, shutting the door behind him.

Devin said, "I put your mail on the desk by your computer so you would be able to find it."

"Thanks babe." Devin pulled her to him and wrapped Megan within his embrace, nuzzling her neck. "I'm tired, hot, and sweaty. I'm going to grab a shower then curl up in bed with you." He lost his train of thought once he gazed dreamily into her eyes. He barely heard her say,

"That sounds like a good idea." Devin kissed her on the forehead and stepped away, walking to the bathroom.

"Hey boss, come take a look at this." Robert stared at the computer screen watching Megan and her boyfriend kiss.

"I'm going to kill that son of a bitch . . . both of them will be dead before long. I hope her uncle didn't get rid of those letters I sent her."

"I'm going to place my plan into action today. Wanna join me? It could be fun man." Robert picked up his camera, and flipped through his pictures.

"I don't know yet if I do or not . . . I'll let ya know before you leave and head out there if I'm coming or not." He smiled, feeling satisfied and happy. His laptop sat next his friend's computer with the camera lens still zoomed in on Megan.

Water stopped draining from the shower in the bathroom, making Megan turn to stare at the closed door and smile. She knocked, alerting Devin.

"Whose is it?"

"Who else could it be silly? Me."

"You can come inside honey." Megan slipped inside, thoughts dancing slowly through her mind of Devin's body, hard, and filled with muscles, up and down every inch of his masculine body. He walked out to the bed and sat down easily, Megan following him.

She sat behind him, resting her head against Devin's back, inhaling his scent deeply. The smell of fresh rain and a hint of old spice enveloped Megan's nostrils quickly making her stomach melt from the heat, swirling within her core. She closed her eyes, sliding her hands slowly from Devin's neck to his chest allowing her fingertips to graze his hard, packed chest.

A high-screeched scream reached her ears, making her eyes light up. Devin and Megan ran out into the hallway, finding her family crowding around the top of the stair case. Millie's body lay at the bottom of the stairs, her body sprawled out; she looked limp like a rag doll. Megan saw blood trickling out of the corner of her mouth, drop by drop spilling into the already large pool of blood forming at the base of her throat.

Megan screamed, her screams penetrating the thin air circulating throughout the house. Tears slowly dribbled onto her cheeks, one by one thinking *this can't be happening all over again!* Clint and Chad ran down the stairs two at a time towards Millie's body. Clint bent to his knees, his fingertips reaching out to his daughter's wrist when Megan shouted,

"No! Don't touch her." She leaned against the railing to stop herself from falling down. Devin stood behind Megan, wrapping his arms around her offering his support.

"But . . ." whispered Clint. He gazed up at Megan in disbelief. Chad grabbed a phone and sat it in his father's outstretched hand. His father dialed nine, one, one and a voice appeared on the line.

"Hello? This is Carrie and what seems to be the problem?"

"It's my daughter . . . she's lying at the bottom of our stairs. I think . . . I think she's dead. There's blood everywhere . . . please I need help!" He shoved his left hand threw his gray-blackish hair and squeezed his eyes shut. When his eyes popped back up, he noticed blood covering the walls of the hallway and blood covering the wooden stairs.

"What's your name, sir?"

"Clint Matthews."

"Where do you live?"

"Pass by 'Country Kitchen' and I live about ten minutes away. Ya'll will come to a road that has a big sign hanging over the driveway and it'll say Matthew Ranch."

"Thank you sir and I am sending an ambulance and police officers over right now."

"Thank you, ma'am." Clint hung the phone up, sinking to the hard-wood floor. His son stood by him and asked,

"Who would have done something like this dad?"

"I don't know son. I just don't know." Clint placed his face in his hands after he answered Chad. Megan stood there in disbelief, *it was Robert I know it was.* Flashbacks plastered themselves in Megan's head, not disappearing even when she shoved her face into her hands, crying, and blocking out everything and everybody. She opened her eyes, staring down at the hard-wood floor, noticing a blood trail showing where her cousin's head had been drug down the hallway to the tops of the stairs.

She raised her head, racing down the hall to Millie's room. The site of the room was too much for Megan. She dropped to the floor, throwing up her lunch. Devin raced over to her, not caring about the blood on his feet or the vomit lying by her. He reached for her, pressing his knees into her lunch, securely wrapping his arms around her. Megan doubled over again, throwing up.

Megan laid her head against Devin's chest, crying fresh, wet tears onto his heavenly scented skin. Her body trembled with anger, hurt, and hatred. Sirens from the ambulance and police cars woke everybody from their trance. Chad and Clint ran outside to meet the ambulance. Shannon followed her mom and two little brothers downstairs, pass Millie's body and outside onto the porch. Devin followed them, carrying Megan's trembling body. He sat down on the steps, rocking back and forth with Megan in his arms. He saw two EMS men go by into the house with a stretcher. One officer stood by talking to Annie, Clint and their two younger sons.

Several minutes passed by before a second officer pulled Chad and Shannon over talking to them. Nobody seemed to notice Devin and

Megan, but he was glad. Meg was still too shocked for any kind of questioning to happen. He sat there, while Megan sat up in his arms and he whispered,

"My sweetie . . ." Her eyes searched his face wanting the relief to know that it was all a nightmare that it hadn't actually settled her eyes upon the two EMS men walking out with a stretcher, carrying a black bag which she knew it contained her cousin's body. The men loaded Millie up into the ambulance and watched them leave down the driveway. She just turned her head to Devin's shoulder, crying her heartbroken pieces out onto him.

He sat there taking every inch of Megan's pain, knowing that she needed him. He held his tears back telling himself that he needed to be strong for Megan and her family. His eyes rimmed red, the gates about to burst. Devin closed his eyes, making the world disappear if only for a few seconds. An officer stood still before him, as Devin shook his head in reply, telling the officer to go away. He bit down on his lips, trying not to cry. The officer patted Devin on the back and trooped away heavily. He looked and saw two and a lady in expensive suits, walking up the steps following the officer into the house. Devin knew who they were, the minute his eyes laid on them. He pressed his forehead into Meg's hair and sniffed her sweet, flowery shampoo. A hint of the perfume he bought for her two months ago drifted to him, pulling his mind and body into its waiting hands.

Sheriff Toby led the three detectives into the kitchen leading to the stairway. He declared abruptly,

"This is where they found the body."

"Who found the girl?" asked Detective Adams.

"Her brother, Chad . . . he heard a thump. He came to check it out."

"Where is his room at?" asked Detective Adams. He wrote the questions and answers in his notebook.

"Downstairs." Detectives Haney and Andrews wrote notes down about the scene at hand.

Haney asked, "How did the blood get here on the walls?" She turned to the Toby and then back to the blood spattered walls and Toby replied,

"Her body was apparently drug from her room, down the hallway, and then I'm assuming the attacker and killer tossed her body down the stairs which would make since about the thump that Chad heard."

"Yes it does." murmured Detective Adams. "Would you take me upstairs?"

"Sure."

"Detective Andrews stay down here and take pictures and notes about everything you see and anything that is suspicious or out of place."

"Yes sir." He walked outside and headed to the car for his equipment. However, Sheriff Toby and Detective Adams and Haney headed up the stairs, trying to avoid the blood. They reached the top of the stairs and saw blood covered foot prints on the floor.

Adams asked, "Now whose feet are these?"

"Mr. Matthews' niece and her boyfriend, Devin."

"Why are their feet covered in blood and why did they run in this direction?"

"That I can't answer but you're going to have to question them yourself."

"Well where are they?" Haney asked impatiently placing her hands on her hips.

"Downstairs missy and don't get sassy with me, darlin'." Toby shut his mouth saying, "Its' just this case is hard for me and my deputies."

"I can understand," commented Adams. He glared at Haney to keep her mouth shut. "The way I see it . . . is the body was drug by the feet allowing the head to drag the floor, leaving the wide path of blood. I'm assuming that she was attacked in her bedroom, we don't know for sure if she was dead yet or not, but she could have been unconscious by this point."

Nothing could have prepared Detective Adams for what he was about to witness. He stepped into the room saying,

"Oh my gawd . . . what the hell happened in here?"

"That I can't answer either," Toby said sadly. Haney stepped into the room following her partner when she smelt vomit. She looked down and saw the smeared pile of vomit at the entrance.

She asked, "Hey did you notice this?" Toby and Adams turned to her and looked down at the vomit.

"I bet it was Megan." The detectives looked at Toby and Haney asked curiously,

"How do you know that if nobody has questioned them yet?"

"Trust me . . . I know my niece, Megan."

"She's your niece? And that little girl that died today was your niece also?"

"Yes ma'am . . . I'm Annie Matthews brother."

Adams declared sympathetically, "Oh I'm so sorry . . . Please us we didn't know. Now I really understand why this is so hard for you and your deputies."

"Yup," was all Toby could say. He whispered, "Excuse me." He pulled out his handkerchief and headed back down the hallway to leave. Haney exhaled deeply commenting,

"Now I feel like a cold-hearted bitch."

"But you're not one . . . you didn't know." Adams stepped further into the room and his partner followed him closely. He stared at the lilac painted walls and the words written in blood. "The Watcher . . . Who the hell is that?"

"I don't know . . ." The bed covered in blood caught her attention. A path of blood led from the bed out into the hallway. The two detectives walked slowly over to the bed and found a small sledge hammer.

"Well we know what was used to bash her head in." Adams pointed out. He hollered, "Detective Andrews!" His other partner appeared at the door clutching bags saying Evidence across the front.

"Need one . . . or two?" As he glanced at the mess before him.

"Please?" Andrews handed them to Detective Haney saying, "Damn. This is one hell of a mess and a shame."

"I wonder why she was murdered. Who would want her dead?"

"I don't know." Clint appeared out of nowhere standing ghost like in his murdered daughter's room saying, "But I bet I know who might have."

"Who?" questioned Detective Adams.

"Robert Anderson."

Chapter Eighteen
SLEEP ATTACK

Robert stepped into his friend's office and set the box containing the payment down on the desk.

"Hey, here's the money."

"Thanks Robert, it's been good working with ya."

"Oh, don't worry it's been the same for me," replied Robert. He sat down by his longtime friend from juvy and commented. "I hope this teaches Megan a lesson." He laughed deep in his throat saying, "I hope my plan scares the living shit out of her."

"Hell I fucking hope it does too."

"All right well I'm going to leave you alone and head back home."

A voice declared sharply, "Miss Matthews and Mr. Scotts, will you follow me inside? My partners and I have some questions for you two."

Detective Adams said, "Megan, were you close to Millie?" Megan raised her head and placed her trembling hands in her lap.

"Yes I was she was like my little sister." Megan's eyes settled on the man sitting before her. Her gaze settled on her uncle, Clint. He stared back with blank, red puffy eyes, the questions never stopping after that. Her mind kept gliding in and out during the questioning.

"Now we noticed the blood stained foot prints on the hallway floor upstairs and a pile of smeared vomit."

"The foot prints are mine and Devin's." Megan inhaled a deep breath, continuing, "I followed the trail of blood to Millie's bedroom . . . and when I looked inside . . . my legs gave way and I threw up."

"I followed Megan and when I saw her drop to the floor, I picked her up and carried Megan down to the porch."

"Um . . . before we go for the night, we have a few last minor questions to ask."

"We pulled your file Megan and found some things we want to know about." She stared at the Detectives blankly and Adams asked, "Who is Robert Anderson?" Her eyes settled on the man in front of her and he noticed the malice coming to life within her eyes.

"Robert Anderson is the man I witnessed against and sent to Juvenile school. He murdered his own sister and spent six years locked away. I moved to my grandmother's house in Atlanta, Georgia. I was always told Robert wouldn't be able to fine me but he did.

"After he found me, I ran away from home and moved here to live with my aunt and uncle and cousins. I have been living he for almost two solid years now and Robert showed up two or three days ago. He is the one who has done this. I know it in the pit of my stomach."

Detective Haney said, "Why did he come back?"

"Your guess is as good as mine. I think he is back for m and supposedly I'm his 'girl' and that he loves me. In my opinion it's a bunch of horse shit. He is obsessed with me because he refuses to leave me alone."

"I see . . . Now Devin, how old are you?"

"I'm twenty." Devin draped his arm over Megan's shoulder, kissing her on the forehead. With the back of her hand, she wiped loose tears from her cheeks.

"How long have you two been dating?"

"Almost two years in two weeks."

"Okay." The detectives stood up, Adams asking, "That will be it for tonight but we will be back sometimes tomorrow."

"Thank you all for your help and we're sorry for your loss." The detectives filed outside, Clint following them. Megan smiled tiredly at Devin as he carried her upstairs past the crime scene up to Megan's bedroom.

Devin laid Megan gently on the bed beneath the covers pulling her close to him. She kissed his chest and rolled onto her side, falling into a troubled sleep.

A doorbell rang loudly in Megan's ears. She flung the door open and Robert stood outside, pushing his way inside.

Megan shouted angrily, "What the hell do you want?"

"Oh sweet Maggie, you're in deep, deep trouble my dear."

"But . . . but what do you want?"

"You!" He snarled at her, his voice filled with malice. Robert grabbed Megan by her hair, yanking Megan's head back making her scream.

"What do you fucking want Robert?"

"You . . . that is what I want Maggie. He released her hair, throwing her body to the floor. Her head coming in contact with the wall. She dizzily stood up, turning for the stairs. She ran for her room, hoping she could find something you could hurt him with.

Robert stood at the base of the stairs, laughing. He shrugged out of his jacket, letting it fall to the floor at his feet. A long, butcher knife gleamed in the light, reaching for Megan as she ran.

"I'm here for you Maggie. You can't keep running from me forever." Megan slammed the door shut, reaching for her softball bat. The door knob rattled, shaking her heart. Then it stopped. Quietness surrounded Megan, deepening the suspense, dragging the minutes onward.

A boot slammed through the door, Megan releasing a scream. She crawled under the bed, praying that he wouldn't find her. His boots stomped around the room heavily, turning to the bathroom desperately looking for Megan.

"Maggie? Oh Maggie where are you? Why don't you come on out, you'll have fun I promise." His voice rang out mockingly, "Maggie. Oh Maggie!"

She gripped her eyes shut, hoping that he would be gone. Two cold hands gripped her ankles, dragging her body against the hardwood floor.

She sat up yelling, "Get the fuck away from me! Stop! Leave me alone!"

Devin wrapped his arms around her as she clung to him her eyes wide open in horror. He kissed her on the forehead and said,

"Megan . . . honey it's me Devin."

She clung to him even tighter, her nails biting his arms. She cried heavily, her body trembling with fear. Her uncle ran in flipping the light on washing the dark walls with yellow. Annie appeared at Clint's side, yelling.

"What's wrong?"

"Megan had a nightmare, sir. She's really scared and I'm trying to calm her down." Megan cried loudly, her eyes glassy with fear. Clint stood next to the bed, placed his hand on her back making Megan cling only harder onto Devin, driving her nails into his flesh. Blood started dribbling down his arms.

He said, "We should probably get her to the hospital."

"I'll go get some clothes on and be right back." Annie and Clint rushed down the stairs to change. Megan's body trembled, her body drenched in cold sweat.

She yelled, "Go away! Leave me alone Robert!" Devin dropped to the bed, picking her up and carrying her downstairs to the awaiting Yukon Denali.

Clint hollered, "Are ya'll in?"

"Yes!" shouted Clint. She spun gravel as she raced down the driveway for the hospital emergency room.

"Robert you are not going to believe this but they just took Megan to the hospital."

"What?" Robert stood behind his friend watching the screen.

"Apparently she had a nightmare and went into shock or something."

"Shit!"

"Yeah I know right." Robert sat down in the seat, wide awake now, rubbing the sleep from his eyes. He peered out the window, slamming his phone down onto the nightstand.

"Shit." He stood staring out the window, anger bursting throughout him. *I need to see Megan . . . I need to see my Maggie.*

Chapter Nineteen
EMERGENCY RUN

They ran into the emergency room and walked quickly to the receptionist. Annie knocked on the glass saying,

"I'm Annie Matthews and my niece . . . well there seems to be something wrong with her. We don't know what it is, but she apparently had a nightmare and we think she went into shock or something."

"Let me come out and take a look at her." The nurse stood up saying, "By the way, my name is Sheri."

"Okay." Sheri opened the door and stepped over to Megan, placing a hand on her arm. Megan broke out into hysteria, shouting. "Stop!"

People in the waiting room sat gazing at that them with blank, curious stares. A nurse poked his head out of the door asking,

"Sheri? Is everything okay?"

"No. Get a room set up immediately for this girl and get one of the docs in there right now to see her." The male nurse appeared and tried taking Megan from Devin's arms but she yelled out,

"No! Stop! Don't touch me!" Megan clamped her hands onto Devin's shoulders and he said,

"Um . . . you might want me to just carry her."

"Okay, but please follow me." He jogged through the open door, leading Devin to an open emergency room. A man in a white coat, stood waiting for Devin. He sat down on the bed, still cradling Megan protectively. He eyed the doctor facing him and he held a shot in his right hand.

He said, "I'm Doctor Chris Butler." He shook Devin's hand and said, "I'm going to give her a shot to calm her down. I need to ask a few questions."

"She had an anxiety attack or as some people like to refer to them as panic attacks. They occur when people get scared really easily."

"Megan was asleep and then at about three this morning, she sat up screaming." He rested his head on Meg's forehead and kissed her feathery hair.

"Did Megan mention anything about what she had been dreaming about?"

"No. All I can figure is that she had been dreaming about Robert." Devin rocked Megan back and forth, humming a sweet tune to her softly. Her grip loosened on Devin as Dr. Butler gave her the shot in her shoulder.

"Now who is Robert?"

"Hang on . . ." Robert laid Megan on the hospital bed, pulling the blanket over her.

"Devin . . . Is Robert gone?"

"Yes baby . . . He is gone, are you sleepy?"

"Yes. Will you stay with me?"

"Of course honey." whispered Devin in Megan's ear.

"Mhmm . . ." She murmured sleepily. Clint handed Devin a shirt, which he put on thankfully.

"Is she going to be okay, Doc?" Uncle Clint questioned worriedly.

"I hope, if I knew what her dream had been about, I could tell you. Has she had anything bad happen to her that could have traumatized her?" Clint's stare flickered from Annie to Devin, resting on his niece.

"Doc, is there some place private we can talk?"

"Why certainly, Mr. and Mrs. Matthews would you two care to join me in my office and explain to me about your daughters' past."

"Well . . . she isn't exactly our daughter." Dr. Butler stopped walking.

"What do you mean she's not your daughter?" He turned and faced them questioning both of them with a penetrating stare.

"Let's go to your office and discuss this privately."

"Would either one of you like a cup of coffee?"

"Please?" asked both Annie and Clint. Dr. Butler led them both down the hall to his office.

Two hours passed as Dr. Butler sat, listening, and trying to wrap his head around Megan's past.

"So . . . you're telling me this girl witnessed a murder, but not just anybody's death, she witnessed her best friend's death. The murderer was her best friends' brother, Robert. She puts him away in juvy for six years and then tracks her down even though she has moved to Georgia, then Megan runs away and shows up on ya'lls doorstep two years ago. Then two or three days ago, Robert hunts her down and is now terrorizing your family."

"Yes sir . . . that pretty much sums it up. Only a few hours ago her cousin, Millie our daughter was murdered. We don't know why, but we believe it's Robert who did it."

"Holy shit, excuse my language but hell. If I had lived the life she has been living then I'd be messed up too. Has she ever been abused by him physically or sexually?"

"No not as far as we know."

"Was Megan ever raped?"

"No."

"Her nightmare had to have been really scary to her if she's like the way she is now." Dr. Butler stood up, glancing out his watch. "I'm going to check on her now then make my other rounds. Care to join me?"

"Yes." He nodded his head and walked down the hall to Megan's room, finding Megan and Devin talking.

"Well how's our patient?" He stepped towards Megan shaking her hand, introducing himself. "I'm Dr. Butler."

"Hello . . ."

"So how are you feeling?"

"Good I guess . . . mostly tired." Devin leaned, kissing Megan on her cheek.

"I'm going to check your IV and I want to listen to your heart." Dr. Butler bent forward placing his stethoscope on her back, telling her when to inhale deeply and exhale. Annie's voice broke the silence.

"Megan, are you hungry?"

"Yes."

"Okay. Clint and I are going to McDonald's and grab some breakfast. We will bring you and Devin some food back."

"Thank you Annie." Megan smiled, thankful of her aunt. Devin continued to hold her hand.

"Megan is it okay if I ask you some personal questions?"

"Sure." Megan watched Clint and Annie leave her and Devin alone with Dr. Butler.

"I want to ask you about your dream . . . about your nightmares."

"What about it?" She lowered her head, hands shaking as she sat waiting and listening.

"Was Robert in your dream?"

"He's always in my dreams . . . well my nightmares. When I first moved here they were frequent. And as these past two years drifted by slowly, I forgot about, not completely but for most of the time I forgot. I always knew in my heart that Robert was lurking around in the dark corners, waiting. Of course he hunted me down and showed back up couple of days ago. He came back on the date of his sister's death. It triggered emotions and memories that I had long time ago forgot about. I resent him and always will. He has been trying to ruin my life for years now."

"I see . . . what was your nightmare about?"

"Let's see here," Megan closed her eyes thinking back, remembering. "I was dreaming I was alone in this huge house. I heard the doorbell ring, I opened it and expected to find Devin, but instead it was Robert." She brushed some loose strands of hair behind her ears continuing slowly.

"He pushed past me inside and I shut the door asking him a question. He was yelling at me and calling me Maggie. He grabbed me by my hair and threw me to the floor. I remember getting up and running to my bedroom, to grab a softball bat.

"I crawled under my bed while he broke my door down, looking for me. Well in my dream, Robert found me, and dragged me out from beneath my bed." Devin's breathing quickened, remembering the horrid, blood-chilling scream that Megan had made.

"I see . . . you had a bad case of an anxiety attack. I'm going to send you home sometime in the next couple of hours. I suggest you rest up in the next two to three days. I'm going to write you a prescription for sleeping pills also." Dr. Butler patted Megan's hand continuing, "I'm going to check on my other patients but I will be back to check on you before you leave."

Dr. Butler stepped out of Megan's room, exhaling deeply, heading down the hall to his office to try and catch some shut eye.

Chapter Twenty
IT'S ALL IN YOUR HEAD

"So where is Megan and your parents?" questioned Detective Adams. He sat at the kitchen table of the Matthews kitchen wondering where they were.

"Megan was taken to the emergency room around three this morning screaming. They should be on their way home soon." replied Chad sipping his coffee, praying that everything was okay. Shannon appeared at the bottom of the stairs, hair rumpled, and eyes all red and puffy.

Shannon sat down nest to Chad at the kitchen table saying,

"Chad? Will you fix me a cup of coffee?"

"Sure." Chad kept his smart ass remark to himself. *What do I look like your damn maid or cook?*

"What are you all doing here?" ordered Clint's voice through the screen door. Clint and Annie helped Devin enter, carrying Megan's sleeping body.

"We're trying to find your killer."

"We all know who the killer is," Clint declared strongly. "The killer sure as hell isn't here." Detective Adams smirked, staring hard at Clint. Devin laid Megan's sleeping body on her bed, tucking her in under the covers. Kissing her ever so lightly on the lips, he murmured,

"I love you." Annie appeared behind Devin asking,

"Are you working today?"

"Yes, I have too and my truck payment is due tomorrow. I'm sorry Annie and I hate leaving like this."

"Its' okay, Devin because we'll be fine here today, so quit worrying about her so much."

"I can't Annie . . . I love her too damn much and I don't want anything to happen to her."

Annie pecked Devin on the cheek saying, "Go to work, clear your head and then come back tonight. She's not going anywhere." Devin carried some work clothes and his boots in his hands down the stairs, rushing for his truck. Annie watched Devin leave, speeding down the driveway, throwing dust and gravel.

Detective Haney asked, "Where is he going?"

"Work."

"Why is he in such a hurry?"

"Devin and his twin, Danny work for their father at his feed mill and work for those boys start at five in the mornin'."

"His dad will understand why he's late, right?"

"Hell no!" answered Clint. "Their father is one of the worst men in this world that you could ever meet. He's the abusive kind and this man has been like this ever since their mother died from cancer when the twins were only three. Chad leaned against the counter, next to his dad."

Clint looked at him, asking, "What happened to you going to Mattie's?"

"I was supposed to yesterday but that didn't exactly happen, now did it?"

"Leave go spend time with her before she heads back to college." Clint ordered tiredly.

"Are you sure dad?" He glanced at his father, wondering what the hell had happened to him.

"Yes, I'm positive. Go to her, she needs you." Clint patted his son on the back, smiling at Chad saying, "Go son." Chad raced downstairs, shoving some clothes in an overnight bag. He kissed his mother on the forehead before leaving.

Annie turned telling the detectives, "I will be upstairs in Megan's room with her."

"I'm going to join you if that will be okay, Mrs. Matthews?" asked Detective Haney following Annie upstairs to Megan's bedroom.

"That will be fine." Megan lay on her side wiping fresh tears away. "Megan, honey what's wrong?" Annie sat down by her niece pulling Megan's head onto her lap, brushing her hair back out of Megan's beautiful face.

"I'm scared Annie."

"Why?" asked Detective Haney.

"Because he's coming for me . . . he isn't going to stop or leave until he gets what he wants."

"Who's coming for you?"

"Robert." Annie let Megan sit up, helping wipe tears away. Detective Haney looked at Annie, frowning.

"Mrs. Matthews declared, "Megan, why don't you get a nice, hot shower? I'll make you some hot tea and we'll leave you to some privacy."

He sat in his black, leather chair watching the screen wanting to get his hands on Megan and complete his famous works on her. The clicking sound of his long, skinny fingers typing expertly away on the keyboard broke the empty silence as he emailed Megan a little reminder.

Hello, Maggie dearest, how are you feeling today? Why did you go to the emergency room? I can't wait to meet you . . . Did you like my little performance the other night? You grow lovelier every day and I would hate to be the one to ruin that little pretty face of yours, just like I did to your cousin, Millie. "The Watcher"

Orange and yellow rays from the descending sun, reached out across the lands, filling Megan's room with light. A phone rang from downstairs somewhere. A gruff, deep voice broke the penetrating silence that had spread throughout the old farm house.

"What do you mean you found something in her skull?" Megan crept to her door, listening to the conversation. "I'll be there in a few minutes. Detective Haney come with me and I'll tell Detective Andrews to stay here with Megan."

She heard the familiar sound of the front screen door banging in the wind as she crept down the hallway to the tops of the stairs, murmuring,

"What does he mean they found something in her skull?"

Detective Andrews stood before Megan informing her that Detectives Haney and Adams left to visit the morgue. She slumped to the floor, fighting back tears mumbling,

"Can things get any worse?"

Chapter Twenty-One
BLACK DAY

Megan crawled into bed later that evening with Devin accompanying her. The detectives had only left minutes before, asking more questions and searching for more clues. After they left the morgue, they came back to the ranch and told the family about the evidence that had been discovered, stuffed within Millie's leftover brains.

It was a letter that nobody could read because it was too badly stained with Millie's blood. The black smeared letters gazed back at Megan, warning her if she did anything wrong, she would end up like Millie or worse. Nobody had to tell her that. She'd already figured that little detail out on her own.

Devin leaned forward, pulling Megan close and kissing her on the lips. He placed a hand behind her neck, arching her head allowing Devin to kiss Megan more fully. She entangled her fingers deeply in his curly hair, pressing her body to his. Devin slipped his tongue into her mouth, moaning with the pleasure of tasting her sweetness. He murmured,

"It's been too damn long since I've kissed you like this."

"I know honey I've missed it too . . . it's just that it's been really rough these last couple of days."

He laid his head on her chest, kissing the tops of her breasts. Devin murmured hotly, "Houston we have a problem."

"What problem would that be?" Devin grabbed her hand and pulled it to the bulge of his briefs making her laugh.

"Oh that problem." He kissed her on the forehead saying,

"I love you Megan and don't ever leave me." He closed his eyes, inhaling her heavenly scent.

"I love you Devin, trust me I'm not going anywhere." She closed her eyes, drifting off into a deep, sleep together.

Seven o' clock blared at her from the radio on her nightstand. She sighed deeply once she realized that Devin wasn't lying beside her, but he was at work. Megan gasped as she gazed out the window, seeing the black low clouds drifting her way. The loud, thunderous booms haunting Megan, making her realize that her own personal storm was just over the horizon.

Her laptop beeped, telling her she had a new message in her Facebook inbox. She read aloud, "Megan I'm warning you that the boogeyman is coming for you. It could be today, tomorrow or next week so be prepared for things coming your way. I hope you like the color black because you're going to be seeing it all day, "The Watcher."

A strange pitter-patter of drops hitting the roof echoes in Megan's ears. It was finally raining after two and a half strong weeks of nothing but heat lighting and the deadly heat. Megan stared at the computer screen in front of her, deciding that she needed to tell somebody. As she passed the yellow taped lines the image of Millie's broken body, lying on the floor in a heap, her throat smoothly sliced open. The penetrating sound of blood droplets dripping in slow motion weakened her stomach.

She gripped her eyes shut, shaking her head, trying to rid her mind of the terrible image. Yet another image came to life before her eyes of another girl dead, her eyes wide open in horror and the last heart-wrenching scream of Abby. Aunt Annie, Uncle Clint and Megan's little cousins sat around the table eating breakfast, gloomily. Clint encouraged Megan with a sad, small smile.

"Come and sit down Megan . . . you too Shannon. You both need to eat." She turned to see her cousin walking slowly towards them as if she was in a trance. Annie declared with a slight quiver in her voice.

"Chad's still at Mattie's and he said that they're coming home around supper time."

"They . . . what do you mean "they"?"

"Chad called me saying that Mattie's stepfather . . . he came home drunk . . . I will just talk to your about it later, but not right now." declared Annie. She stood up walking outside, letting the screen door bounce in the wind.

"Okay . . ." murmured Clint. "Anyways, Annie and I are taking the boys to go stay with your Grandma Thelma for a few days. We believe it would be for the best for them right now."

"Okay."

"So you two are in charge of the house while we're gone."

"Yes dad."

"Yes uncle." Clint bent across the table, kissing both his girls on the forehead and left. Annie stood out front at her vehicle waiting on Clint.

"Would you want to spend today together?" asked Shannon, sipping her coffee quietly.

"Yes." Megan stared at Shannon, offering a weak smile. "I think that would be nice."

"I vote we watch a movie." Shannon and Megan ran into the living room, putting on one of their movies, "Grease".

The window slid open without much force as rain beat on his back, the whispering winds pushing at their bodies. Thunder roared, surrounding each of them in light as lighting crackled loudly. Each of them slithered their bodies through the window, landing on the hardwood floors with a loud thud.

Shannon's gaze locked on Megan's asking,

"Um . . . please tell me you heard that?"

"I heard it too." Shannon paused the movie asking nervously,

"What do we do?"

"I have no idea . . ." Megan grabbed the remoter from her cousin saying,

"It's probably just the wind or the thunder because our nerves are jumpy as it is."

"Yeah you're probably right." Shannon murmured to herself.

Minutes ticked by, before another loud thud came from upstairs, joined by a third thud. Heavy breathing filled their ears slowly, increasing. The girls stared at each other as Shannon's eyes grew in wide in horror. She whispered to Megan.

"Did you hear that?"

"Yes." Megan replied shakily. "I think someone is behind us." Her heart quickened beating rapidly against her chest making the pain increase.

Shannon reached for her cousin's hand, gripping Megan's hand in her own. The heavy breathing, burned hot against their necks. Megan willed herself to turn around and look. A man stood behind them in white washed blue jeans, black t-shirt while his face was painted raven black. A butcher knife gleamed at the girls as he whispered,

"Boo." Shannon and Megan jumped up, screaming. Three more identically dressed men appeared behind the first. Megan's adrenaline running so fast she thought her heart was surely to stop any minute.

She screamed furiously, "What do you want?"

"Hmm . . . that's an easy answer because there are two young beautiful girls, standing here all alone without any parents, boyfriends, or friends to protect them. We want you two of course and since there aren't enough girls to go around, I guess the four of us will be sharing you two."

"No! Stay the fuck back!" Megan reached for a glass off the wooden coffee table and threw it at him. He moved out of the way, letting it hit the wall behind him with loud shattering noise.

"Hold up missy . . . we haven't committed any crime yet."

"Yes the hell ya'll have . . . breaking and entering, being on private property and . . ."

"What else because that shit isn't enough to keep our asses in jail."

"You're . . ." A cold, hard gloved hand slithered around Megan's waist, gliding up under her thin, tank top while the other hand gripped her throat as the fingers curling around her skin, digging into her flesh. A harsh, hot voice murmured in her ear,

"Give me the gun and nobody will get hurt."

Megan put her hands in the air as Shannon walked backwards against the wall, wailing,

"Stay the fuck away from me! Don't touch me!"

One of the now five guys picked Shannon up, flinging her body over his shoulder. "Put me down!"

Megan stood helplessly watching as the man ran off with Shannon while two of the guys followed after them. The man holding Megan slithered his hand up under her sports bra, grabbing her right breast saying hotly in her ear, "You're mine."

She closed her eyes thinking *oh shit . . . they're going to rape us and then kill us!* He pushed her forward and ordered, "Walk." She did as she was told because she could hear Shannon's rough, loud screams from upstairs joined with the shouts of the men yelling.

Seeing it as her one and only chance, Megan kicked the guy holding her arm in his already hardened manhood, running straight for the screen door. She ran head first into the piss pouring rain, heading straight for the barn. Her fingers gripped the rungs on the wooden ladder, hauling herself up to the loft, squeezing her body in between square hay bales.

Her cousin's shouts and screams of protest echoed from the house, stilling Megan's blood, slowing her heart. Megan bent down on her knees, praying that Shannon and herself would make it through today. Rosie's bark filled the air, warning Megan that the men were coming for her. She shoved her fist into her mouth, muffling her cries.

Rosie's barks increased, getting louder and harsher. A shot ran out below Megan, the barking deceased. *They shot her, they shot Rosie!* Heavy footsteps creaked up the ladder. Megan knew they were coming for her. She closed her eyes, rocking her body back and forth, softly.

One of the men shouted, disgustedly, "We have to find her ass for the boss because that little bitch is going to pay for kicking me. I'll show her who I am."

Their heavy footsteps crept closer towards Megan as she sat frozen in fear listening, not knowing what to do. She looked up to find one of the men standing before her, his eyes filled with malice. The men's eyes blazing white against their black painted faces.

Each of the men grabbed Megan by her arms, pulling her body from the hiding spot. They laid Megan flat against a column of hay. The man, who Megan had kicked, roared at her.

"Do you think you can just kick me and get away with it? Hell no bitch!" He swung his hand around coming in contact with her nose. Her head rolled to the side, as his fist hit her stomach. He wrapped his thick, strong hands around her throat, squeezing tightly.

She laid there gasping for air, only exhaling, receiving no oxygen, only punch after punch to her ribcage from the other guy. The man with his hands corralled around Megan's throat continued to squeeze. Her eyes bulging out of their sockets and off in the hazy distance, she heard the sound of a truck pulling up. The men dropped her body to the floor making Megan crumble up into a bal. She laid there in a heap, sounds rolling in and out of her ringing ears while her vision kept blurring in and out. She closed her eyes, blackness surrounding Megan, dragging her body into its deep, dark depths.

Chapter Twenty-Two
YOU WILL PAY

The rain pounded against the windshield, as Chad's truck rolled up in the driveway. He turned to look at Mattie, saying softly,

"We will go inside, find Shannon and Megan and we sit down and watch a movie with them. Okay?

"Okay." Mattie answered nervously. Chad smiled at his girlfriend, twisting her long, fiery red locks around his fingers.

"Let's go inside." Chad helped Mattie's weak body into the house, trying to beat the pouring rain. He set her bag on the floor in the kitchen saying, "make yourself at home darlin'." He grinned at her, thinking *where are the girls?*

"Megan! Shannon! Where are ya'll?"

Chad turned and saw the television still on in the living room, the bag of spilled potato chips, and the table of magazines spread out across the floor. "Mattie . . . Honey stay here okay? I'll be right back." He reached for the butcher knife, but found it missing. "Shit!"

He reached over Mattie, searching for the shotgun hiding behind his father's office door.

"Stay here Mattie. Please!" He stepped around the yellow tape, climbing the stairs two at a time. He peeked into Megan's room, and didn't find them. He crept down the hall to Shannon's room, swinging his arm and body around blocking the entrance, holding the gun firmly within his hands.

Shannon's body lay wrapped and twisted within her lime green sheets, her head sticking out. Her head slowly turned her mouth open gasping for air.

"Help . . . me . . . Chad." He pulled out his cell phone dialing nine, one, one as he crossed the room to his sister.

"Hello. This is dispatch. How can I help you?"

"This is Chad Matthews and I need an ambulance right now!"

"Where do you live?" He repeated his dad's words from days ago. He pressed his hand to Shannon's forehead, asking,

"Shannon! Who did this to you?"

"I don't know . . . there were three men." His eyes questioned hers, pressing his hand to the side of her head. He yanked his hand back as he touched a warm liquid.

He stared at Shannon's head and saw the gash. The red liquid seeped from her skull soaking her pillow. He looked down and saw that blood soaked stained her sheets from which she was entrapped in.

"Where did they go?"

"I don't know . . . did they get Megan?"

"Megan . . ." He shook his head shouting, "Where is she Shannon?"

"I don't know Chad."

"Shit!" The wails from the sirens of the ambulance and police officers, screamed. He ran downstairs meeting the same EMS men who came for Millie's body days ago. "Follow me!"

He led them upstairs to Shannon's bedroom. They strapped Shannon onto the stretcher leaving her body entangled within the sheets. Clint and Annie's black SUV parked next to the ambulance, as the rain became nothing more than a light drizzle.

They loaded Shannon into the back of the ambulance speeding away down the driveway. The sirens wailing in the distance darkening the afternoon. Clint and Annie ran over to Chad and Mattie yelling,

"What in the fuck happened to Shannon?"

"Hell if I fucking know! I just pulled up about ten or fifteen minutes ago. I was looking for the girls and I found Shannon like that," shouted Chad. "She said that three men did that to her." Clint muttered a stream of curse words.

"Fuck! Where's Megan at then?" yelled Clint. He ripped his hat off throwing it into the wind.

"I don't know!"

"Hells bells! Do you know anything then boy?"

"Yes I fucking do, *dad!* We don't know where she is!"

"Shit! I bet you anything that bastard Robert did this!"

"I bet he fucking did too!" Chad ran his fingers through his blonde curly hair asking, "Hey where's Rosie?"

"Rosie!" hollered Annie, crying. Mattie walked down the porch, joining Chad.

"What's that?" questioned Mattie, pointing at a heap at the entrance of the barn,

"Rosie? Rosie!" yelled Clint. He ran over to the barn, Chad and Mattie following him. Clint dropped to his knees beside Rosie's dead body yelling, "Those fucking assholes killed my wife's dog!"

"Who would do something like that?" commented Officer Andy. Chad stared down at the soft, soupy mud by Rosie and saw a small fraction of a footprint.

He said, "Dad! What does that look like to you?" Clint stared at what his son was pointing out and answered, hope filling his eyes.

"A footprint . . . Megan!" Clint and Chad stared at each other running into the barn. Chad quickly climbed the ladder, knowing immediately where to find Megan. She always hid there when they played tag or hide n seek.

"I think she's up here!" The cops stood at the base of the ladder, waiting. As Chad approached the last row, he heard shallow breathing. Megan's body lay on the loft floor, chest barely rising or falling. "I found her!" Clint stood behind his son lifting her into Chad's arms, making their way carefully down the ladder. He laid Megan down on the ground, her heart barely beating. Megan stared back at Chad through already swollen, bruised eyes grunting.

"Men . . . five."

"Shush now you're safe. We found Shannon and she's at the emergency room."

"Rosie?"

"Um . . ."

"Dead." Megan's head rolled to the side, her breath coming in and out as uneven gasps. Chad stared at his cousin's neck and saw the bruised marks of fingers digging into her flesh. *Robert you're a dead man.*

Robert stared at the screen, loving what he was watching. He laughed deep in his throat, revenge and hatred on his mind.

"Hey, Robert . . . I'm wore you, you've kept me busy this week."

"Good but you're not done yet."

"Oh goody! Who's next?" questioned his accomplice rubbing his hands together, smiling gleefully.

"You shall see," Robert smirked murmuring. "I'm going to pay you extra for today."

"Hell yeah!" He leaned back in his chair, resting his feet on the edge of the desk, snarling. "Oh by the way, Shannon tasted sweet. Her blood on my tongue was music to my body."

"You're sick."

"I know but tough shit and just remember who went looking for whom?" Robert left shaking his head.

Chapter Twenty-Three
TWO DOWN

Officer Andy beat on Robert's front door shouting, "Hello? Is there a Mr. Robert Anderson living here?"

"Yes and he is coming." Robert walked to the door and opened it saying, "How may I help you?" He leaned against the door frame.

"We think you might be able to help. Would it be okay if we came in?"

"Oh yeah sure, come right on in out of the rain. My place isn't the cleanest apartment, but I try." Robert replied innocently.

The officers walked around, looking at everything and anything. They nodded their heads in approval. One of them whispered,

"He's not our guy, we're looking at the wrong man." The men searched the rest of his apartment, not finding one shred of evidence that might link him to the Matthews family. As they walked back to the kitchen to join Robert, he was sitting at the bar, eating a salad.

He looked up asking, "What service can I be to ya'll?"

Mike answered, "Where were you two mornings ago and where you this morning?"

"I was here at home watching a baseball game and having breakfast. After that I read the local newspaper and watched a movie." replied Robert.

"Then I ate, went to the football field over at the high school and ran a few miles."

"Is there anybody that can testify or better yet prove that you were there?"

"Yeah, now that you mention it, my cousin Stacey Anderson was with me."

"Okay, thank you. We got work that you paid a visit to a Ms. Megan Johnson. Is this true? You know that she has a restraining order against you, now we asked Chad Matthews and he told us that you were crossing the line, just a reminder."

"Yes sir and thank you sir." Answered Robert playing his cards right.

"We're going to go now and we may drop in every now and then to check up on ya."

"Got it," Robert smiled at them.

"Now ya have a night ya here?"

"Yes sir and you officers do the same."

"Bye now."

"Bye." Robert eagerly said, wanting to get rid of them. *Man that was a close one. I almost didn't make it back home in time. I just hope they don't go searching for Stacie because they aren't going to find her.*

Megan sat on the bumper of an ambulance, barely able to see anything. She murmured, "How long will it take for this swelling to go down?"

"Oh, probably a good few days. Why?" asked the EMT, Sissy.

"I was just wondering . . ."

"So you don't know who did this to you sweetie?"

"No . . . but I have a hunch I know who it was." Megan said angrily.

"Okay. Before I take off, is there anywhere else on your body hurting?"

"Yes, besides my face and neck, I'd have to say my sides and stomach. My ribs are hurting mainly on my left side." Sissy lifted Megan's tank top and saw what she meant.

Sissy said, "Honey I'm afraid I'm going to take you to the hospital for x-rays. Let's get you loaded up." She helped Megan get situated in the back of the ambulance, slamming the doors shut. Sissy joined Chad, Mattie, Clint, the officers and the three detectives saying, "Mr. Matthews I'm taking Megan on to the emergency room to get x-rays and a full check up. I think she has some broken ribs."

Devin's truck lights sailed across everybody standing in the driveway with broken, pained expressions covering their faces. He put the truck in park and ran over to Chad asking, "What the hell happened here?"

"Apparently five men broke into our house, raped Shannon, beat her skull in, and tortured her. Megan was able to escape the other three men. She hid in the barn but was found and then they beat her too."

"Where is she?"

"Megan's in the back of the ambulance they are taking her to the hospital because Sissy thinks that Megan may have broken ribs." Devin rushed to the ambulance, speaking hurriedly to Sissy. She nodded her head and let Devin climb in the back with Megan. His eyes landed upon Megan and his heart shattered to pieces.

He whispered, "Megan, my poor baby. What happened to you?"

"Devin is that you?"

"Yes, honey . . ." His voice trailed off as he wrapped her into his arms. He said, "Baby I'm sorry I shouldn't have left you all alone today by yourself. Will you ever forgive me?"

"Devin it wasn't your fault. I wish I could see your face." She ran her hands over his familiar face and smiled through a split lip.

"I'm going to find whoever did this to you and your family and I'm going to make them pay." Devin declared with vengeance.

The ambulance rolled up next to the emergency room doors with Megan securely strapped to the stretcher, they rushed her inside, with Devin following in hot pursuit.

Devin planted a strong, loving kiss on Megan's lips. He strolled out meeting Dr. Butler in the hallway.

He asked Devin, "Hey, what brings you here?"

"Megan."

"Uh oh, why is Megan back in here?" Dr. Butler asked alarmed. Devin led Dr. Butler into Megan's room and he asked, "Just out of curiosity, do you have a cousin by the name of Shannon Matthews?"

"Yes."

"I just got done evaluating her and all I have to say is what the hell happened to ya'll?"

Megan answered weakly, "Somebody broke in well more like five men dressed in black shirts, blue jeans and their faces painted black so neither Shannon or myself could identify them.

"Whoa," Dr. Butler said shaking his head. "Sissy informed me that your ribs are hurting you?"

"Yes." Megan ran the tips of her fingers over her face, feeling the puffiness of her swollen eyes and her split lip.

"I'm just going to raise your tank top up enough to look at your ribs.

"That's fine." Dr. Butler reached for the hem of her tank top and observed her ribs, pressing on the spots bruised more than other spots.

"Does that hurt?"

"Yes." replied Megan biting her lip to hide the pain.

"I'm assuming you're in pain?"

"Like hell I am."

He rubbed his eyes saying, I'm going to send you down to the lab to get x-rays done."

"Thanks."

"After that you can go home and I don't want to see you in here again for a long time."

"Funny." answered Megan lamely. "I highly doubt if that will work."

"We will see about that." Devin sat down beside Megan, taking her face in his hands, kissing her face.

"I love you and I think it's time we went on vacation, just you and me."

"Sounds like a plan." Megan giggled and Devin laughed back at her, loving her laugh.

"Hi, Ms. Megan, are you ready for your x-rays?"

"I guess so." Two nurses along with the help from Devin, they were able to get her into a wheelchair.

Devin commented, "I'll be right here if you need me okay? So when you get back, I'll be here waiting for you."

"Okay." She kissed him on the cheek muttering, "I'll be back soon." Devin walked next door to Shannon's room waiting on Annie and Clint to arrive.

Chapter Twenty-Four
DATE NIGHT

The Matthews' Ranch remained quiet for the next three days allowing a dark silence to erupt throughout the house and its members. Megan sat at her mirror, looking at herself for the first time in days. The swelling from her eyes, started reducing, but the bruises on her neck, were taking their time to fade away. She applied chap-stick to her lips, noticing the slight silver of a scar.

Snoring filled the empty room and her ears, making Megan turn to see Devin still asleep in bed, right where she had left him. She smiled happily, turning back to the task at hand of wrapping her ribs up securely. The pain was slowly diminishing, her ribs feeling better each day. Thinking about that Monday, brought clear images to her head.

Megan's cousin, Shannon remained in the hospital. They were finally moving her out of critical care today, because she wasn't slipping in and out of consciousness. The loud snores stopped and strong callused hands curled around her waist.

She said, "Good morning Devin." He bent forward, kissing her on the forehead.

"You're looking much better today sunshine."

"Thanks," She closed her eyes thinking about Monday again and the looks of the men's eyes burning through her skin, twisted her stomach in fear. "Are you going to work today?"

"I don't know, I think that it's still too early to head back yet."

"Okay. Do you want to go into town with me?"

"Sure, then maybe we can stop by Susie's Ice Cream Parlor and grab her famous ice cream cones and watch a movie back here at the house?"

"Yes sounds good to me darlin'. It's just I need to get out of the house for a few hours and get my mind off things around here because me being on lockdown twenty four-seven isn't helping."

"I know well then let's get out of here." He kissed her squarely on her cute, small lips. Megan met Devin at his pickup truck and cuddled up next to him, thinking back to the first day they met. She laughed softly. Devin cocked his head to the side, glancing back and forth from the road to Megan.

He said, "What's so funny?"

"Nothing babe, nothing at all." She kissed him on the cheek, still smiling. The rain stopped barely above a drizzle. Devin smiled at Megan kissing her nose in the sprinkling rain, listening to her laughter filled Devin's heart with pure joy. The wind whipped playfully at the hem of Megan's dress. She grabbed the edge of her hem in a fist, trying to keep it from sailing up around her.

Robert threw his hood up over his head letting Devin and Megan pass as he exited the barbershop. He pulled a cigarette out, lit it, and dragged heavily on it. Tiny, droplets of rain descended upon him. He looked down the street and saw them enter the ice cream parlor.

"Megan's marks on her neck are better than I had pictured. The men did a good job on her but I think they went a little too far with Shannon. Oh hell who cares? I sure as hell don't."

Megan turned as chills crept up her spine slowly. A strange but familiar man stood in the middle of the sidewalk, his mouth supporting a freshly lit cigarette. Devin pulled on her hand, Megan whipped around forgetting about the man watching her. She couldn't shrug the feeling away that she was being watched, but by who?

He climbed the stairs lazily, watching Megan, his Megan from across the street eating ice cream with Devin.

"Where did I go wrong with Megan? What mistake did I do to make her hate me so much? I wish she could see that I love her and always have."

Robert smirked, his insides cringing with pain when he watched Megan's lips touch Devin's. Anger swam within his veins, hatred boiling deeper and deeper. He gritted his teeth, wanting desperately to end this battle.

Chapter Twenty-Five
IT'S TIME TO PAY

Megan sat at the table later that evening trying to eat supper with Devin but mostly played with her food. Clint sat next to her, kissing Megan on the cheek asking,

"How are you holding up?"

"Fine, I guess." Megan leaned back in her seat, watching Chad ease himself into the seat across from her. She leaned up on her elbows asking,

"How's Mattie doing?"

"Better . . . she's asleep right now."

Clint commented, "Your mother never got a chance to tell me what happened this morning." Chad closed his eyes thinking *should I tell them or wait until Mattie's awake? Ah hell I'll go on and explain everything to him.*

He stared at his father muttering, "You would ask me that wouldn't you? Well I stayed the night at her apartment over her stepfather's garage. You remember hose her mom passed away about two years ago, well her stepfather wasn't home but that morning he broke down the door, came running in her room, found Mattie and me well . . . you can figure out the rest." He cleared his throat, trying to be a man about Mattie's and his sexual life in front of his dad.

Megan choked drinking her coffee and Devin patted her back saying,

"Cough it up girl." She grinned at Chad making his ears turn beet red with embarrassment.

Devin commented humorously, "Please continue Chad. I have to hear this." He laid his fork down and stared mockingly at his best friend, crossing his arms.

"Well as I was saying . . . Mattie and I . . . well you get the damn picture. Anyways, he broke in, found us, ripped her off me by her hair, dragged her naked body out into the living room, and threw her against the wall."

"I took a chair and broke it over his head. He dropped to his knees and I picked Mattie up carrying her into her bedroom. We both got dressed and I helped her pack her bags. The whole time we're packing he comes in her room shouting, 'get your ass out of my damn house whore!' She broke down into tears and slammed the door in his face. We got her things she mainly wanted and we left. Just to let you know, Mattie's isn't ever going back, our plan is for Mattie to keep going to college and then I'm going to start taking night classes while I work during the day. We plan to get married next spring and I hope you agree with my plans and believe that I made the right decision."

"Hell no son, I would have killed that son of a bitch. I will stand by your side with whatever decision that you make. I guess this means you're going to start looking for a decent piece of farm land for ya'll."

"Yes, sir . . . that's the idea. The wedding isn't going to be elegant or elaborate either because we both just want something for the family, and a few close friends. Oh yeah there is one other thing."

"What's that? It's not like she' pregnant or anything, right?" Clint laughed at his own comment. When Chad didn't answer directly he asked, "She's not is she?"

"Dad . . . I wasn't exactly planning to tell you this until later next week but um . . . I hope you want grandchildren." Chad leaned back in his chair watching his father' s facial expression, watching it change from surprise to angry back to surprised.

"Chad, I've never been more proud of you as I am today! Congratulations! How long has she been pregnant? Is it going to be a girl or a boy?"

"Dad calm down, we didn't want to tell you and mom because we didn't want to alarm to ya'll. She is almost a month long and we go to the doctor next week. We won't know the sex of the baby until a few months later on down the road." Clint stood up, hugging his son and kissing him on both cheeks. He ran for the house phone and hollered,

"I'm calling your mother and telling her!" He ran out onto the porch and sat on the swing with his coffee in one hand the phone pressed to his ear. Chad sat back down, with a big smile plastered to his face. He stared at Megan and Devin saying,

"What do you think?"

"Chad this is big! I'm going to be an aunt? Chad . . . congrats!" She ran around the big table to her cousin and wrapped him in her arms. She kissed him on the forehead and said, "I'm going to make Mattie a baby blanket. Can I go see her and see if she's awake?"

"No, she's sick. Let her sleep please?"

"Why of course!" Megan sat back down next to Devin, bouncing up and down with joy.

Devin said, "I'm so proud of you Chad. I hope I get the part of being best man."

"You will don't worry and Megan seeing as how Mattie doesn't have any brothers or sisters, she was kind of wondering if you and Shannon would want to be her bridesmaids. Devin is going to be my best man and once the baby is born we want you two to be the godparents."

Megan exclaimed excitedly, "Of course we would love to be the godparents!" She hugged Devin and he shook Chad's hand saying,

"Thanks and guess what this means?"

"What?"

"I get to plan your bachelor party!"

"Oh no the hell you aren't! Danny sure the hell isn't because he'll want to get my ass roaring drunk and I'm diffidently not going down the aisle or to my wedding hung over so forget that shit, it's not happening Devin." explained Chad knowingly. He grinned devilishly at Chad.

"I'm going to go upstairs okay? I'm going to get ready for my date with you on the couch, watching a movie. I had Chad pick me up a movie last week and it's a surprise. I haven't watched it yet, but I've been wanting too."

"Yes dear, whatever you command." He said playfully. He swatted her on the ass as she walked away.

Megan reached for her computer, hearing the soft pitter patter of rain on the metal sheeting roof. Signing onto her Facebook page, she saw two new messages one from Millie and a second one from her unknown messenger.

Reading aloud her unknown messenger's email,

"Megan, how's your face? I hope it still hurts and I hope you liked my little performance the other day with your cousin. She desperately deserved what happened to her. You have no idea of what's going to happen to you once I lay my hands on you. Just you wait baby, you're mine! I'm upset with you though so it's going to cost you, are you willing to pay the price?"

She sat there stunned and decided that it was time to write this sick twisted freak back. She wrote, *Dear The Watcher, what the hell do you want from me and my family? If you're all cracked up who you say and think you are why didn't you just already kill me and take what you want? Don't you think you've taken enough from me already? What more do you want? Who is this by the way? Why do you keep playing these stupid, pathetic little mind games for? If you're a man and if you think you're got the balls to perform these cruel, sadistic acts, then I don't think you're man enough to do shit, Megan.*

Megan pushed the send button, leaning back into the chair thinking *I feel much better since I got that out of my system.* "I'm going to have Devin take these to the police station because I'm tired of this shit."

She printed out the saved letters from her computer she stood up and went back downstairs, finding Chad, her uncle and Devin in deep conversation. Megan said,

"Excuse me, but um . . . I need to borrow Devin for a few minutes."

"Okay." He stood up and walked her way, Megan asking,

"Will you take these letters down to the police station for me because I've been receiving letters from somebody that I don't know and I think they are from the guy that has been terrorizing our family."

"Of course sweet pea because once I get back, we're going to have our date that I have been promising you."

"Sounds good to me Devin." She stood up on tip-toe and kissed him firmly on the mouth. She slipped her hands around his neck as Devin pressed his body to hers, letting his fingers dig within her hair, commanding her body to arch against his.

Uncle Clint hollered, "Calm it down in there! I maybe old but I'm not that old for grandkids!"

Devin released Megan, walking away from her outside to his pickup truck ready to leave for the police station. She giggled, falling against the wall, touching her cheeks liking how warm they felt. Taking two steps at a time, Megan raced up the staircase to her room remembering that she had left her window open. Her phone rang, breaking the sound of rain slashing against the house.

"Megan speaking . . ."

"Hey babe, it's Devin. I'm sending Danny over to offer a little bit more back up at the house."

"Sure. You are taking those letters straight over to the police station aren't you?"

"Yes babe, so don't worry your pretty little head." Devin teased playfully.

"Thanks." Megan laughed softly into the phone saying, "See ya in a bit. I love you."

"I love you too baby."

The chair squeaked at Robert as he leaned forwards in his chair, listening and watching the conversation of Megan talking on the phone.

He shouted, "What? Wake up man! Come on I need you on this one." He hit his friend on the arm, waking him up.

"Who am I killing this time?"

"It might be Megan before too long but listen to me. She printed those emails that you have been sending her and someone is taking the letters to the police station for her but I don't know who. I think it's her cousin, Chad but I could be wrong. We have to put our final plan into action now because this might be the only chance we get."

"Let me call her, I got this under control."

"Fine . . . you do that and see if you can get any information from her." Robert's accomplice dialed Megan's number, blocking his own.

Megan's hot pink phone vibrated in her hand. She answered, "Megan speaking?" Heavy breathing dragged her back to the morning of the break in and the five men. "Hello?"

"If you call the cops or tell anybody about those letters, you're a dead woman."

"To late asshole because, you know what? He's already on his way over to the police station." The line clicked dead. She stared at her phone knowing that she just shared words with the man who murdered Millie.

"So . . . you don't have any idea on who might have written these emails to your girlfriend?"

"No sir, no idea and the only person I can think of would be Robert." explained Devin sitting on the edge of his seat.

"You know what? I'll have an officer run over to Mr. Anderson's apartment and check things out." Toby yelled out the door at the older looking cop as he stepped in the boss's office.

"Yeah boss?"

"Go check out Robert Anderson's apartment and if you find anything suspicious and I mean even one pair of women's panties or a picture of Megan or Millie or Shannon bring his ass in. Plus, those murders could be linked to him."

"Hey, what about that Willie guy? He lives close to Robert."

"Bring his ass in also because both these guys have a record."

"Wait . . . who is this Willie guy?"

"Son, let me tell you he is one bad mother fucker. He's got a record that would scare the shit out of ya." Toby held up Willie's record asking, "Wanna take a look?"

"I guess so." Toby tossed Devin the record, saying,

"I hope you don't have a weak stomach." Devin scanned sheet after sheet, finally coming to pictures. He threw the file back onto the table shouting, "Holy fuck!"

"Do you think she really will go to the police?" questioned Robert's friend.

"It's a possibility but then ya never know with Megan. If she's smart then she won't."

"You are going with me right?"

"Hell yes because I don't want to miss this for the world. I'm going to clean out my apartment and get my shit packed in your truck."

"Okay. I will be here, just be back here in ten or fifteen minutes."

Chapter Twenty-Six
HIDE AND SEEK

Chad climbed the stairs to his cousin's room and saw Megan sitting by her window, just staring off into space. He smiled to himself, walking over to her carefully. He stepped on a floorboard, making it creak under the pressure of his weight. Megan spun around, alarm locking into place across her face and fear seeping into her eyes. She spotted Chad and let out a gush of hot air.

She said, "Next time don't scare me like that."

"What are you scared that the boogieman is coming for you?" He pulled a chair up beside Megan saying, "Are you okay?"

"Yeah surprisingly I'm doing alright. So what happened to Shannon exactly? Nobody has really told me anything except that her skull was beaten in just like Millie's."

"Well when I found her, her skull was crushed in, bleeding of course and she was wrapped in her sheets naked. The sheets were soaked in blood. One of the guys took a knife and cut little slits along her arms, stomach and legs and her back. Then each of the three men that were with Shannon raped her." Tears developed again, she wiped them away quickly with the back of her hand. Chad wrapped her in his arms saying,

"Hush now because it's all going to be okay. Don't worry Megan, I promise we're going to catch this guy."

"It's just something has me stumped."

"Let me guess it's the letters right?" replied Chad with a smile.

"Yes."

Danny rushed inside, declaring, "Where's the party at?"

"There's no party man."

"Chad can you come here for a minute and bring Danny down with you."

"Sure dad! Be right there!" yelled Chad. "Well we'll get out of your hair." He smiled forcing Megan to smile back. She watched them leave smiling. As Megan stared out her window, seeing a figure out at the barn created a funny feeling that crept to her stomach. The cell was holding vibrated in her hand.

"Megan speaking,"

"Megan I know what you did. You sent that boy to the cops. Plus Robert just called me saying that the cops showed up his apartment looking for him again. What fucking game are you playing at? Trying to get Robert blamed for shit that he didn't do?"

"I should ask you the same damn thing! You're not my fucking friend. Get a life and stop screwing up mine!"

"Guess what?"

"I can see you right now." Megan spun around feeling eyes staring into her backside but nobody was standing there behind her.

"If you can see me right now, then where the hell am I?"

"In your bedroom, close to your window and there are two chairs next to the window where you and Chad had been sitting and talking only moments ago." Megan stepped away from the window, sitting heavily on the bed. "You're now on the bed."

"Where are you?"

"You'll see my dear, don't worry . . . but here's a question for ya, do you like hide and seek?"

"No. Why?"

"Well you've just entered the house of mind games. Sit back, take a load off your feet, and relax. Ready to play?"

"No . . ."

"Ah that's too bad, so here we go? Question number one, what makes this noise?" Heavy breathing appeared on the line and she blurted out.

"A human?"

"Correct but whom?"

"What do you mean who is it?"

"Answer the damn question!" Megan thought *oh my gawd, he has Clint or Chad or Danny. Which one is it?* She ran her hand across her face, breaking out into a light sweat.

"Am I allowed any hints?" She closed her eyes, crossing her fingers, praying that he would say yes.

"You are allowed only two hints." Her eyelids flashed open mouthing, yes.

"Sure. Who found Rosie lying dead in front of the barn?"

"My Aunt Annie?"

"You're wrong darlin' but guess what? Clint say your good-byes!" The crushing sound of bone, transmitted through the pone speaker. The last gasps of life drowned out Megan's thoughts. Life ultimately felt drained from her body, like the last shreds of hope were sucked from her soul, never to return.

Her body numbed quickly, a wretched sound filled her ears. Megan didn't recognize the noise at first, but the shrill sound of a chainsaw echoed slowly through the speaker. Horrid images of her uncle filled her mind. Megan collapsed, falling backward onto the bed.

A voice filled the speaker saying, "Gota call ya back, I've got a bleeder on my hands. Ha-Ha!" Megan continued lying on the bed, scared to move. Her phone started vibrating, she answered.

"Are you there?"

"Yes." Megan mumbled hatefully.

"Question two, what is this noise?" A terrifying scream filled Megan's ears.

"A man screaming,"

"Correct, now let's see if you will do better this time? Who has a baby on the way?"

"Chad!"

"Correct! Hey Chad, guess what? Today is your lucky day because it's not your time to die today. You get to live, marry Mattie and have your baby, but I'm going to leave you with a present, a reminder of me." Ear splitting screams radiated through the cell phone. Megan's memory screeched to a halt while numerous sounds escaped the phone, directed at her.

A cold voice filled the line, advising Megan to stay on the line if she wanted him to keep his last captive alive.

"Are you comfy now?"

"No!"

"Here's another question, who told Robert about you moving here?"

"Joe?"

"Yes ma'am! He sold you to the devil!" He laughed cruelly, the pieces of the puzzles starting to fit into place.

"Hey, Devin! Say your last prayer and I hope you don't have any sins that you haven't confessed to yet. Good luck in hell, but it's not all that bad. I survived and if you don't want to end up like me, then pray to the good Lord that He forgives you! Say bye to Megan!"

The line clicked over dead, stirring pain, freshly made twisting and spiraling throughout her veins heading first class towards her heart making love diminish into pieces, hatred being replaced.

"Are you there?" The creep asked evilly as Megan answered her phone.

"Fuck you." Megan murmured softly.

"Hang on because I promise you that this next event is going to rock your world."

Black clouds raced outside, turning the sky completely black. In Megan's heart, she already knew her personal storm had only arrived moments ago, coming to claim her.

"Do you like hide and seek games?"

"Kind of . . . Why?"

"Good luck Megan!" sang the voice on the other line. The lights flickered off making Megan whisper softly.

"Fuck." She heard a loud knocking noise, hoping that it was somebody to save her but her hopes vanished, running back to the shadows. She realized that she had been hurled into one of her worst nightmares. Robert stood but only inches apart, declaring harshly,

"Poor little ole Megan, all alone this time and nobody here to save her! What will poor little ole Maggie do?" He grabbed Megan's hair within his fist, throwing her body to the floor.

Robert stomped over to Megan, grabbing her by the throat, picking her body up off the floor, and slamming her against the wall. He let go, letting Megan fall in a bundle of limbs at his feet.

"Stop!" Megan screamed at the top of her lungs.

"No!" ordered Robert. He squatted to his knees laughing in her face. "Run and hide Megan. I will give you a few seconds start, I promise. One . . . two . . . three . . ."

She jumped to her feet as quickly as her body would allow her. Megan made it up the stairs, slamming and locking the door shut. Loud footprints trailing up the stairs stopped at Megan's bedroom door. She crawled under the bed, hearing Robert yell.

"Maggie . . . Maggie come out and play with me!" Seconds ticked by, the lights continued to flash on and off, no longer scaring Megan, only the empty silence threatened her. Robert's boot kicked through the wooden door. She pressed her hands against her mouth, trying to muffle her startled screams.

"Maggie? Oh Maggie where are you? We aren't going to hurt you, I promise." She watched as his boots stepped closer to the bed, towards her closet. The lights flickered off completely. The dead silence crept to Megan, sucking her into a world she no longer desired to be a part of anymore. Cold, strong hands grasped her ankles.

"Found ya!" He dragged her body out from underneath the bed, flipping Megan onto her back and pressing her body against the hardwood floor as tears streamed down her face.

"Stop fucking crying! You're not four are you?"

"No." mumbled Megan weakly.

"I found her, she was almost too easy to find." A man stood over Megan making her insides twist and knot upon laying eyes on the man calling himself, "The Watcher."

"I figured, are you ready to leave?"

"Yeah, if you are."

"I got my business here taken care of." Robert said, looking back at Megan. "Are we going to leave the lights on?"

"Hell yes because it will only make my performance more interesting. I have always learned that if I'm going to go down, I go down with a bang." said Robert's friend smirking at Megan.

"I think it's time we give you a taste of your own medicine." Robert slipped a needle into Megan's arm, her eyelids slowly falling forward second by second. Robert picked her limp body up, throwing her over his shoulder, carrying Megan out to the truck, tossing her into the backseat.

"Willie, let's go before the cops show up."

His friend sped down the long driveway, pulling out onto the main road. Instead of going through town, they raced to the interstate.

Chapter Twenty-Seven
KEEP GOING

Devin traveled the Matthews gravel driveway, wanting to get back home to Megan. Images flooding his head of Megan's smile, her soft hair. He smiled as he drifted closer to the house every light blazed through the windows. He thought *what the hell happened?*

He parked the truck close to the barn spotting a figure lying by the steps on the porch. He shouted,

"Hello?" Hearing no reply, he jogged to the body curiously lying on the ground. The lights shined down, engulfing the lump of human. Devin realized that it was Chad. He stood but inches away gasping at what lay before him, what was left of Chad anyways. He bent down pulling the duck tape and bandana away from his mouth. Chad inhaled deeply, sucking in as much oxygen as his lungs would allow him too. His face black and blue, his nose cocked to the side and his throat lightly slit.

Chad murmured painfully, "Devin . . . help!" Devin pulled out his old razor cell phone and dialed nine, one, one. He explained to dispatch that his friend was in desperate need of an ambulance. He pushed the phone back into his wrangler jean pockets. Devin made himself look at Chad's body, trying to figure out what the hell had happened to him. Chad was shirtless, showing where Willie had taken a knife and cut deeply into his chest, carving his name. His jeans ripped in several places and barbwire was twisted and tangled around his body tightly. The metal claws digging into his bare skin, little by little every movement he attempted.

Devin said, "Let me go get some wire cutters and I'll get this shit off you!"

"No!" hollered Chad with every inch of energy he had left stored in his body. "Go check on Mattie!"

"Where's Megan?"

"They took her, they kidnapped her!"

"Who?"

"I don't know who . . . I'm sorry."

"Let me go find Mattie . . . but where is Danny and your dad?"

"I think . . . they're dead." Hearing those words knocked the breath out of him. Devin stood dizzily swaying in the hot air murmuring,

"I'll be right back."

The screen door lay against the siding of the house torn from its hinges. Devin grasped the wooden door handle and felt something warm as it smothered his hand instantly.

Devin reacted, pulling his hand back and stared at his worst fear, blood as it smothered his palm. A round object hung nailed to the door, while his eyes roamed higher, locking on the culprit of the blood. Clint's head, stared back at him. He fell backward against the railing, his hands clutching the post in his hands until his knuckles turned whites.

The reeking stench of Clint's head rotting in the heat mixed with the blood tore at Devin's stomach. He flipped his head to the side, vomiting. He wiped his mouth on the sleeve of his t-shirt. Devin pushed the door open allowing the light to shine down upon Clint's face. His eyes bulged out in horror while his mouth hung open, tongue less.

Blood smeared the kitchen floor leaving a trail to the refrigerator. Bloody fingerprints smudged the handle, giving Devin the idea to look in there. In a Tupperware bowl held Clint's tongue, fingers, and toes. Devin slammed the door shut, not wanting to continue. He found the stairs leading to the basement hoping to find Mattie, unharmed.

He shouted, "Mattie? It's Devin where are you?"

"I'm in here!" Maggie hollered back. She beat her fists against the door, wanting to get out of the dark closet.

"Mattie I have to move this dresser out of the way." He flung the door open Mattie falling into his arms. He steadied Mattie on her feet saying, "Don't come upstairs please? I beg you, please stay down here. I don't want to go upstairs because it's a fucking massacre. Stay here until the cops show up."

"Okay." Mattie murmured scared. She crawled onto Chad's bed whispering, "I'll stay here."

"Thank you." Devin ran back upstairs, knowing that he had to continue searching the rest of the house for Clint's remaining body parts. Deep within his heart, he knew Danny his twin was dead, but he needed to find the proof to end this antagonizing fear building up within his body.

As he passed Megan's door, his heart sank once he laid eyes upon the broken door pieces. His chest ached, all he wanted to do was just fall to the floor and give up but Devin continued. Fresh blood spattered the walls in Shannon's bedroom with the name "The Watcher" smeared in Clint's blood. Lying on the bed was Clint's intestines, flies swarmed around the mess, trying to find which piece was most delicious.

Devin closed his eyes and walked away heading towards Millie's room. His eyes roamed the room, searching for anything out of place. His gaze locked onto the dresser and shoved into each drawer was his toe and handless remains, sticking out at odd angles. Blood streamed into a waterfall of redness, creating a large pool of thickening blood. Wails from the sirens of the ambulance sliced the heavy silence as Devin ran downstairs meeting EMS.

He stood by Chad's body pointing and shouting, "Over here!"

"Holy shit!"

"What the fuck happened?" The two EMS men lifted Chad onto the stretcher, strapping him down tightly, only pressing the barbwire deeper into his flesh. Chad winced, biting his lip trying his damn hardest not to yell out.

Sheriff Toby shouted, "Damn! It was that fucking bastard Willie!"

"Shit!"

"Where's Clint?"

Devin turned saying, "You really wanna know?"

"Fuck yes!" Toby shouted, placing his hands on his hips staring Devin down, intensely.

"Follow me," Toby flashed Devin to the door pointing and saying harshly, "There's your brother in law." Toby stared, his jaw hanging open in horror.

"Where the fuck is the rest of his damn body?"

"His tongue, fingers, and toes are in the refrigerator. Then his legs and arms are upstairs in Millie's dresser. His intestines are lying sprawled across Shannon's bed and I'm not even going to mention where the rest of his dismembered body parts are." Toby sat down heavily, in a trance of terror, trying to let everything seep in at once.

"Where's Mattie?"

"Downstairs . . . she was locked in the closet, but I let her out and we have two bodies unaccounted for."

"Shit! Like whom?"

"Megan and my twin, Danny."

"Fuck! Damn that son of a bitch to hell!" shouted Toby pissed off.

"Devin!" hollered one of the deputies.

"Yeah?"

"We found Danny's body!" Devin ran after Toby to the barn. Lights shined down on his hanging brother's body. Devin dropped to his knees, at his brother's feet dangling in mid-air. His twin's face twisted in fear. His hands were nailed to the upper level of the barn. Danny's head split in two, barely recognizable as blood stained his skin, flies buzzed around in complete serenity.

Devin dropped his head into his hands, while his heavy tears shook throughout his entire body. Toby stood there next to him, with his hand pressed to Devin's shoulder, understanding his pain.

Chapter Twenty-Eight
YOU ARE MINE

"Willie she's starting to wake up." Trees passed, turning black as nighttime quickly approached. Cars' lights brightened as the numbers decreased the longer they drove. "Give me another one of those shots." Willie handed Robert the shot as Megan's vision blurred, seeing figures hazily moving around in front of her.

She murmured drowsily, "Where am I?"

"You're safe Maggie, go back to sleep." Robert shoved the needle into her arm, squirting the clear liquid into her veins. Megan's head rolled to the side, falling onto Robert's leg. His fingers slid through her hair, liking the way her hair caressed his rough fingers.

"Is she back asleep?" Willie asked, turning around to glance at Robert and Megan.

"Yes."

The truck turned to the right turning down an old driveway hidden by trees overgrown from years of abandonment. Stars, shined brightly upon them as an old, white decayed farmhouse came into view.

"I'm going to go toss Megan into a bedroom, then I'll be back to help unload the truck."

"Dude! Why the rush? Take all the time you need."

"Not yet."

"All right." Willie turned his back stepping out into the heat, liking the familiar feeling of being back at home. Robert slid out of the backseat, dragging Megan's drugged body out of the truck. He slung her over his shoulder and headed up to the house. He waited for Willie to unlock the door.

"Are you sure you don't want to stay with her?"

"I'm sure Willie." Robert stomped up the staircase and tossed her body into the first bedroom. Megan laid on the bed, her dress flowing around her long legs. His gaze roamed over her legs, letting his fingertips dance gracefully against her skin.

He stared at her as desire rippled throughout his body while voices yelled at him to take what was rightfully his. Her lips, luscious and pink, dared him to what he desperately been longing to do for years. Robert placed his hands on either side of her head, his body hovering over Megan's. He bent down, placing his lips to hers, letting his tongue glide against Megan's lips playfully.

Inhaling and tasting her scent, drove Robert over the edge. He sat down beside Megan, putting his hands on her bony hips, dragging her body to his hungrily. Megan opened her eyes slowly realizing what was going on. She put her hands firmly on Robert's hard chest pushing him away from her. His fingers circled around her wrists, pushing Megan against the bed. He straddled her waist moaning her name softly.

He said hotly, "I want you Megan." Robert pulled Megan's wrists above her head trapping her while his other hand slid beneath her dress cupping her breasts. Robert moaned again, pressing the bulge of his jeans against her thigh. Lights disturbed the darkness as Megan's cries of protest filled the silence. Her eyes wandered over to the door where Willie stood watching happily. Robert leaned back on his heels shouting,

"Willie get the fuck out right now!" He pointed toward the door and Willie laughed at him, slamming the door in Robert's face. His laughter echoed throughout the house, sending cold chills up Megan's spine.

Megan lay on the bed, trapped beneath Robert's body as he straddled her hips. He yanked his shirt over his head tossing it to the floor. His boots and socks joined the shirt. Robert stripped his jeans off, standing before Megan in only his boxers. She stared at Robert wide-eyed, fear rushing throughout her body. She slid her legs and feet under the dress, waiting nervously for his next move.

"Come here." Robert ordered aggressively.

"No." mumbled Megan.

"Maggie! Come here."

"No Robert! Leave me the fuck alone. Please just leave me the fuck alone!" shouted Megan breaking into tears. He crawled onto the bed and reached for her ankles under the dress dragging her body to him.

She wailed desperately, "Stop! Stop it Robert!"

"No, Megan! You are mine and always have been mine." Robert pressed his mouth to hers but Megan wasn't having any of it. She whipped her head to the side, making him kiss her cheek instead. A hand snaked around Megan's neck, fingers digging into her scalp, gripping a fist of her blonde, curly locks and jerking her head back.

He said, "Megan the more you fight me, the angrier I'm going to get and rougher." Robert held her head in place as his tongue slid into her open mouth, seizing control. His lips traveled down to her plump, perky breasts. Robert smirked at her, as he tasted her soap and inhaled her perfume strongly. It swam like a toxic disease to his brain, roaring throughout his blood stream.

"Stand up and strip, now!" ordered Robert.

"No!" His hand came in contact with her cheek, his ring grazing her cheek, slicing the skin open. Blood trickled down Megan's cheek.

He murmured, "Fuck! Look what you made me do Maggie." She shrank away from him, running to the window. She rattled it, trying to open it but nails and wooden boards sat in place destroying any shred of hope of escaping. Robert grabbed Megan by her hair, throwing her to the floor. He yelled hatefully at Megan.

"I'm fucking done with you and your games Megan! You either strip for me or I'll do it for you because either way you're mine Maggie!"

"Shit! Stop calling me Maggie!" screamed Megan. Robert reached over to his jeans, stood over her haggard body, and placed a gun in front of Megan.

"Now which is it going to be?" Megan whimpered, giving in, knowing that she had been beat.

"Put the gun away . . . I'll do it." She clumsily stood up and walked nervously over to Robert. He tossed the gun to the bed, holding his hands up. "I'll do what you want . . . just don't hurt my family anymore than you already have." Megan lowered her head, dropping her gaze to the floor. "What do you want me to do?"

"Strip!" Megan stepped away from Robert and walked miserably to the bed. Robert's eyes followed her to the bed. She stood with her back to him unzipping her dress slowly, as his eyes followed the zipper. Next she pushed the straps over her shoulders and let it drop to the floor in a pool of color. Megan reached her hands to her back, unclipping the bra letting it land at her feet. Megan remained standing her head half turned to Robert watching his eyes violate her body.

He whispered huskily, "Continue."

Megan bit her lip as she slid her hands to her hips, pushing the white lacy thong down to her ankles, letting it join the other discarded items of clothing. Robert's eyes burned a smothering black, as they roamed over Megan's body. He left trails of burning flames across her skin.

He walked to Megan, wrapping his arms securely around her. Robert's strong, rough hands capable of murder traveled up and down the length of her body, touching gently. His hands warm but cold did what they pleased. Robert closed his eyes and breathed heavily in her ear. His lips seized her mouth, pressing his tongue against hers, toying with her, trying to make her take the bait. Megan did and she knew later on she'd regret it. He picked her up, placing her on the bed lightly watching her hair flow across the pillow.

Robert pulled his briefs off and curled up next to her. His hands left her hips, floating to her breasts. Playing with Megan only intensified his fantasy.

He murmured, "I want you Maggie right here and right now." Tears formed against her eyes knowing that nothing would ever be the same anymore. Megan blocked everything out and disappeared into a world of a complete dark and empty world, a place she could only go.

Chapter Twenty-Nine
ROUND TWO BEGINS

Megan's eyes roamed the room, afraid to move, frozen in trepidation. She stretched her arms feeling the coarse ropes tighten on her wrists. She squeezed her eyes, shut as hatred clawed at her heart, wanting to fill that empty void.

Her fists gripped the pillow, squeezing with all her might. Megan shifted her legs as the cold sheets rubbed against her skin reminding Megan that was naked. Devin's face appeared within her mind arousing fresh tears. She gulped them away, not wanting to think about him or her family members. Darkness from the room swallowed Megan whole, dragging her body to its cold depths from within.

Robert disappeared downstairs buttoning his jeans walking bare footed down the wide, wooden staircase feeling the coldness from the wood seeping into his skin. He followed the hallway down to the kitchen, hearing the noise from a flat screen television set making Robert wonder if Willie was asleep or not. He peaked around the corner into the living room and saw Willie drinking from a beer bottle and watching a movie.

He whistled asking, "Do we have any food around here?"

"As a matter of fact we do. Follow me my good friend." Willie climbed out of his dad's old lazy body recliner leading Robert to the kitchen. "Have whatever your heart desires."

"I'm pretty sure I took car of that already." Robert replied laughing at Willie making him slap Robert on the back, smirking.

"Yes, Robert I know I heard and by the way where is our guest?"

"Lying upstairs on the bed tied down to the mattress where she belongs." Robert replied proudly. Willie laughed loudly asking,

"Want a beer?"

"Hell yeah! I thought you'd never ask."

"Here," Willie tossed him a cold, Coors light saying, "I'll be in the living room if you need me."

"Okay." Robert pulled a frozen pizza out of the freezer, tossing it into the oven. He leaned against the counter, smiling humorously and feeling quite pleased with himself. He ran his tongue slowly against his teeth, tasting Megan's sweetness and purity. He savored the moment with Megan, only enticing his desire for more.

Light slithered across the room slowly followed by heavy footsteps crossing the room in a hurry. Thoughts raced throughout Megan's head. The touch of a stranger jolted her stomach, making it twist in fear. Her heart quickened as fingertips traced her spine down beneath the covers, seeking her skin. A hand pulled Megan onto her back so she wasn't lying on her side anymore.

"Are you ready for round two?"

"No." Megan whispered tiredly. Her voice crackled from her throat being so dry.

"Answer me!"

"No!" Megan shouted hatefully. Her inner core cried out in pain, malice only deepening.

"That's much better," Megan heard the familiar noise of jeans unzipping and the rustle of them being pushed down her legs. Robert crawled under the sheet, pressing his naked body to Megan's. He whispered playfully, "I missed you and I'm ready for you."

"Well I'm not." mumbled Megan under her breath.

"Bitch. You better watch your mouth." Robert said harshly. his eyes roamed proudly over his prize. "I'll be easy with you but I can't promise anything."

"Like hell you won't." He slapped her ass, jerking her had back saying,

"Woman I told you don't sass me!" Roberts slid his hand to her thigh, squeezing and inching higher. She sunk back into her private, black world already knowing what was going to happen.

Megan pushed all her other thoughts away, waiting and wanting to go on and get it over with so he would leave her alone for awhile. The scent of hard liquor drifted to her nose, making her stomach contents rock.

Chapter Thirty
ESCAPE

Devin sat at the police station thinking about Megan and how he wanted his life back together. Tiredness swept him to his feet pulling him out of Toby's office. He let the sheriff know that he was heading home to get some sleep.

Toby stood in the aisle watching Devin walk outside wearily, heading to his truck. Toby closed his eyes, grabbed his hat, and passed Amy, his secretary. He told her that he was going home to his wife and that she had better not call him unless it was a dire emergency. Toby walked out front of the police station dragging his worn, ragged body to his cruiser and drove home. Amy shook her head, praying that things will change for them.

Annie laid next to her daughter, Shannon in a bedroom at her brother's house watching her sleep peacefully. Shannon's bandages around her neck glowed in the moon, pouring silently into their opened window. Her hair had been cut like a boy's, the black stitches blaring against her skull, filling Annie's heart with dread and hate. She murmured against Shannon's shoulder,

"Where are you Megan?"

Her eyes flashed to the door, wanting somebody to come and let her out. Megan didn't care about anything or anyone else at the moment, only herself and escaping. A light thump of footsteps on the stairs stopped outside her door. The door creaked open irritability, cutting the thin silence.

"Maggie, are you awake?" questioned Robert.

"Yes."

"Do you want to go to the bathroom or get something to eat?"

"Yes."

"Okay well get up." Megan slid out of bed and stood with the white cotton sheet wrapped securely around her body.

Robert said, "I'll get you some clothes and put them in the bathroom for you." He led her across the hall to the bathroom as pain radiated through her legs as she followed Robert across the hall.

She shivered, drawing the sheet tighter around her worn, bruised body. Robert laid a slinky, black gown on the sink counter making Megan sigh tiredly, dreading what her future might lay ahead if nobody found her.

He declared sharply, "I'm going to let you have some alone time, but after that you're mine." In his hand he held a black, lacy bra and a black lacy thong. "Here you might want to come eat in a few minutes."

"Hmm how thoughtful." murmured Megan. He grabbed her by the throat, squeezing hard enough to remind her of what he was capable of.

"Watch your mouth, Megan darlin'." Her eyes watered from the pain shooting through her body. She bit her lip trying hard not to scream at him. Robert let go, her body falling to the floor. She coward against the wall as Robert slammed the door in her face.

"Bitch." mumbled Robert heading downstairs to join Willie and wait for Megan.

Water drained down her body, soaking the white carpet beneath her feet. She glanced at the newly bought lingerie and groaned. Megan pushed her arms through the skinny straps and mumbled,

"I look like a prostitute."

"Well honey that's because you are mine." He smirked at Megan and laughed humorously. "Follow me." Robert led Megan to the kitchen a water bottle and food sitting, waiting for her. "Sit down and eat."

"Fine." Willie walked in, his eyes landing on Megan. She studied Willie trying to understand where things went wrong.

"Were you ever in jail?"

"Sure, hell I spent most of my life in and out of jail. Not to mention the mental institution that my parents booked me in."

"Why?"

"Cannibalism." Water spewed out of Megan's mouth across the table. "Seriously?"

"Yep when I was around twelve I think." Willie answered with a smile. Megan swallowed her food twice to keep it down. "When I emailed you those letters, didn't you ever take my warning into consideration?"

"No, not really." She shoved some pizza into her mouth, hoping that he'd quit asking her questions.

"Well you should, because I can always ruin that little pretty face of yours."

"Whoa, I'm scared." mocked Megan. She rolled her eyes at Willie.

"She doesn't believe you," said Robert.

"Yeah well I'm going to prove her wrong. How about I take her into my work shop and mess with her a little bit?"

"No, not yet but wait a little bit longer."

"Okay. I hope your uncle enjoys hanging headless from the front door."

"What are you talking about?" Megan ate the last of the pizza and swallowed.

"Like I said, I hope your uncle enjoys hanging from the front door."

"You . . . you cut his head off and hung it to the front door?" questioned Megan, staring at Willie with a blank stare.

"Yeah and I also amputated the rest of his body and intestines, stringing them around the house." Megan sat there, listening carefully to Willie. Vengeance and repulsion soared throughout Megan's veins. She jumped out of her chair, knocking it back and letting it fall with a slam to the hardwood floor. She attacked Willie, her nails digging into his face. Robert grabbed her and yanked Megan's arms behind her back.

Willie yelled, "Bitch you will pay for that!" Robert carried Megan upstairs throwing her body to the floor shouting.

"Stay here and calm the fuck down. I'll come back and check on you later." He stomped out of the room, slamming the door behind him. Megan ran to the door and peeked out into the hallway. She didn't see anybody so she took this chance as her one and only time to escape.

Megan positioned her body against the white walls, creeping down the stairway slowly. Stopping on each step, waiting, and listening closely to each creak, every moan, every little whine raised Megan's level of alertness. She crossed onto solid ground, standing still and listening to the old grandfather clock ticking away, wasting minutes. She pulled the door open slowly, squeezing her eyes shut, waiting for somebody to hear the door open, but nobody came.

The wind pushed at her skimpy gown, gluing it to her bruised body. She tip-toed down the stairs, running straight for the barn that lay ahead of her. Fresh bailed hay raveled itself within Megan's nose seizing control of her. She sighed deeply, wandering into the moon lit barn. Praying that she could find someplace to hide, before they discovered she was gone. The tool room was filled with a warm, soft glow pulling Megan only deeper into the room.

She placed her foot on the concrete step, stepping in something sticky. Smeared thickly on the hard, concrete floor was one of her many worst fears. The smell of hay was drowned out by the stench of rotting meat. Looking around slowly, her eyes wandered across the walls, gazing in horror at all the hand tools drenched and stained in blood. Megan clasped her hands to her mouth, smothering her cries and screams.

A metal door stood tucked away within the walls, barely visible. Megan pulled the door aside and locked the bolt in place. She crept inch by inch to the back corner. Holes in the metal door allowed light to barely stream in. Meg wiped wet, salty tears away and laid her head against the wall. The room felt stuffy, sending waves to her head, her thoughts slamming to a screeching halt into one another. She curled her legs up to her chest and she laid her head on her knees wanting to just be alone and hide.

Robert relaxed on the couch, stretching before standing. He read the clock on the wall and whispered,

"I think I'll go check on Megan." Images poured into his mind of Megan. He walked upstairs, laughing deep in his throat but his smiled diminished once he found Megan gone. He shouted in frustration, "Megan!"

Willie appeared at the bottom of the stairs asking,

"What's wrong?"

"That bitch ran away!"

"Fuck."

"Tell me about it! Go check the barns and the sheds. I'll check all over the house."

"Deal."

"I want her back so I can personally kill her with my two bare hands!"

"Hey I thought that was my job."

"Just go fucking find her." Willie ran down the stairs, rushing outside to the barn. Heat surrounded Willie as he stepped into the barn but a light from his tool room raised his curiosity.

"I thought I turned it off." Willie steadied his pace as he walked inside, stepping on the blood. Willie's lip curled up into a half smirk, as he grinned. Hunger drove him, wanting to taste fresh meat on his tongue. His senses flared, upon smelling a scent that stuck out.

He exclaimed, "Oh Megan? Where are you?" He reached for a butcher knife hanging on the wall beside his head. He sneered knowing where she was the moment his eyes locked on the metal door tucked away in the far corner. He grinned happily, standing before the door.

"Oh Megan, I know where you are."

Chapter Thirty-One
THE HUMAN DOLL

A voice filled Megan's ears harshly, waking her up. She sat straight up craning her neck towards the door, her eye peering through one of the holes. Willie dropped to his knees, placing his nose against a gap, sniffing the wondrous scent of a female, the scent penetrating his nostrils, burning the hairs with a deep desire. He closed his eyes and grabbed his chest, feeling his heart beats quicken.

Megan fell back against the wall as a nose filled one of the holes, then an eyeball. The eye swiveled around its socket, searching for its prey. His heart beat rapidly to a different rhythm than most human hearts. Willie spotted Megan, his voice declaring sweetly,

"You smell so damn delicious and I can't wait to sample and appetizer." Willie's human soul left his body replaced by his demon, knowing already that he was in for a mouth watering treat. "Why don't you come out and play with ole Willie for a chance?" He pounded on the door with his fist demanding that the door open.

Megan yelled furiously, "Fuck off!"

Willie stopped, knowing exactly what kind of tool was needed. She brushed her loose hair back, behind her ears. Tears swelled hotly against her eyelids. The sound of chains clinking beat her ears. The noise deceased followed by a dead silence. The rippling sound of chainsaw, roared to life suffocating Megan's screams. She flattened against the wall as teeth from a chainsaw reached for Megan, crawling through the metal door.

He dropped the chainsaw, killing the engine. He grasped the metal door while the raw edges clawed through his hands, ripping his skins' seams apart. Willie stood before Megan glaring.

"I'm going to teach you a lesson" He pulled Megan off the floor by her long, curly hair out into the blinding light. The soft, warm glow of the lamp betrayed Megan only luring her closer to the predator at work. Never was she going to be blinded into a situation like this ever again. Megan's feet dangled in the air as her nails dug in his white flesh.

A silver, metal medical table hung in mid-air before Megan as she screamed. Her screams floated to his ears, calming and pleasing Willie's body, only sucking his sadistic personality into clearer view. He slammed her body on the table, allowing coldness to seep throughout Megan's body slithering across her skin, playfully. Lying on her stomach he chained her ankles to the table's edges.

The raw metal cut into Megan's skin as blood dribbled down her already blood coated feet. He reached across his victim's body chaining her hands to the table's edges above her head only increased Willie's fantasy of seduction, but not in most men's way of thinking. His way of seduction was beyond most of his gender's thinking capacity, it was pure and fresh. Willie dropped to his knees, laughing cruelly as he stooped to her level his blue eyes blaring into hers ominously.

Willie murmured cynically, "Are you ready to play? Which tool should I use first?" He held up a butcher knife, a drill, and shards of glass. Thoughts explored Megan's mind, blueprinting layouts of possibilities. She forced the tears to stop shouting,

"Fuck off!" He threw his head back, laughing. Willie walked to her legs, grabbing her small left thigh. His fingertips ran up to her inner thigh, pulling the thin materials' hem over her butt, exposing Megan.

"Your blood and meat is going to be a glorious treat."

"Leave me alone!" His fingers reached under the thong strings, cutting the black material off his captive's body. He picked the drill up, pressing the button allowing the shrill sound to break the silence. Willie placed a long, grey screw against her leg, pressing the button once again.

Her skin twisted under the pressure of the screw, as it raveled itself within her flesh. Blood squirted droplets at Willie making him sigh. Megan's hideous screams dominated the air, ceasing the sound of the drill.

Pain swallowed Megan's veins, capturing her heart, squeezing and draining the life out of her.

He placed a plastic bowl under her leg, capturing the flow of the blood. His mouth watering anxiously, wanting to have a taste. He dipped his index finger into the blood, allowing his skin cells to imprison it. Willie's finger traveled to his mouth, his lips curling around his finger.

The taste satisfied Willie exciting his taste buds. Megan's screams flooded his ears.

"If you don't stop screaming I will drill more screws into your body. See if I give a damn about whether you live or not. I'd rather go on and finish my work on you. There is no telling how many women's bodies and girls bones are scattered around this farm."

He smirked and walked around the table to Megan's right thigh, setting up another screw. The drill bit twisting the metal into her thigh producing Megan's screams. Throbbing pain seared throughout Megan's body like hot venom, as it sailed its way, eating her nerves alive. Willie placed another small bowl under her other thigh, not wanting to waste any.

"Have you learnt your lesson for today?"

Megan peeked out through her sore eyes, landing on Robert's muscular frame as he leaned against the wall. He strutted over Megan, grabbing a fist of her hair, pulling her head back. He planted a kiss on her swelled, bloody lips as his tongue grazed down her jaw across the base of her throat.

He whispered huskily in her ear, "If you ran away again or try to escape, I'll let Willie here get his hands on you again and perform his famous works on you."

Robert released her hair, letting Megan's forehead hit the table with a loud, thud. He stood by Willie saying,

"Thanks for catching her. I think I can take it from here."

"Should I leave screws in her legs and arms?"

"Hell, why not?" smirked Robert.

"Hang on . . . before you go I have one more thing I want to do to her." He ripped Megan's black gown, letting the torn pieces fall gracefully at her sides.

"What are you doing?"

"Just watch and you will see." Robert crossed his arms, his muscles bulging under the strain of his shirt. He watched Willie grab a small, glass shard and set it straight upon Megan's back and pushed with all of his might. The piece of glass sliced her skin and cut deeply into her back.

Megan bit her bottom lip and her teeth dug into her lip, blood streamed down her lips, dribbling onto the cold, hard table. She closed her eyes, blocking out the pain with all her might, the throbbing evaporated into numbness. She squeezed her eyes shut as more pieces of glass were pressed into her back and left there.

Sweat covered Willie's face as he stepped back to admire his work for the day as the pieces of glass spelled Robert's name across her shoulders. He slapped Willie on the back, impressed with his work yet again. Robert declared approvingly,

"I think it's my time that I have some fun with her now."

"Go for it because I've had my fun for the day." Willie's eyes locked on Megan's back as the blood crawled downward forming fresh pools of blood at her sides. Willie and Robert released their captive's arms and ankles, while they hung limp in the air. He picked his bowls up telling Robert.

"Help me tilt the table so I can get the rest of Megan's blood into these bowls." His eyes followed the pool of redness as it slid into the plastic bowl. Megan groaned as pain rippled throughout her body at every little movement. Willie sat the small bowls in the refrigerator near the medical table.

"Let me clean up down here and then I'll be up there soon."

"Okay." Robert slung Megan's unconscious body over his shoulder and walked back to the farmhouse leaving a trail of blood following them as they climbed the stairs to the bedroom. He slammed the door shut behind them saying, "If you ever try to run away again, I will let Willie do much worse."

His hard, chiseled skin pulled tightly against his face as he clenched his jaws shut. His eyes staring hard into hers' as he tossed Megan onto the bed. Robert shrugged his jeans off, standing naked in front of Megan. Robert stretched out beside his capture, loving the way her soft skin felt against his. Megan watched callused fingers tip-toe up her legs, his rough hands slide up and down over her ribcage. Blood roamed over Megan's already blood stained back, crossing over into new territory, claiming Robert's hands.

The strings from the gown slipped over Megan's shoulders revealing her bruised skin to him and to him alone. Robert tossed the discarded ruined clothing item to the floor. He whispered hoarsely,

"Come here." He pulled her body into his arms and draped his leg over Megan's trapping her. He pressed his head against her head, sniffing her hair. Robert sighed, saying, "You will want me."

"No, I won't."

"Oh Maggie yes you will."

"No."

"Yes, oh yes you will Maggie." He smiled kissing her forehead continuing, "Roll over on your stomach." Megan closed her eyes, feeling his hands on her legs pushing them into the position he wanted. She sniffled, trying to hide her tears, already knowing what was going to happen next to her.

Chapter Thirty-Two
ON THE MOVE

She laid there letting Robert do what he wanted, as he sighed deeply out of pleasure, and closed his eyes. Megan squeezed her eyes shut, tears rolling drop by drop from the corners of her eyes, falling rapidly onto the pillow. Screams erupted from Megan's mouth as pain shot through her body from Robert.

"Please stop Robert!" She shouted loudly.

"Shut up." He ordered, concentrating on Megan and the task at hand. *Please let somebody come find me, I can't take much more of this.*

Mr. Johnson sat in his sister and brother-in-law's kitchen at the table, listening to every little detail that had occurred in the last two weeks.

"I'm sorry for all the pain and trouble that I caused for ya'll. I thought I was doing the right thing by letting my daughter runaway and live here with Clint and you."

"I don't even know what to say to you Dave," muttered Annie. She sat staring at Megan's dad thinking. Megan's father shoved his head into his hands and sat there, not knowing what to do anymore. Toby walked in and eased his tired body in a chair beside Annie.

"We're doing our damn best to catch these assholes." Toby stared blankly at his coffee mug saying, "Why would Robert follow Megan all the way down here and go through all this damn trouble?"

"He's a nut and so is his friend, Willie Miles."

"I know that but still when I lay my hands on him . . . on Robert he's so dead."

"Tell me about it but both of them are dead, Toby."

"Yeah, Willie really made a mess of Annie's and Clint's house."

"Shit!" Mr. Johnson leaned back, tension still building within his soul and body. He exhaled slowly.

"Well he lit the fucking house up like a damn Christmas tree."

"So I heard . . . Annie, how is Shannon?"

"Better, you can go upstairs and see her if you want." He stood up, pushing the chair back. He headed for the stairs, looking in each room, searching for his niece. When he found her, his heart froze in beat of time. Toby stared at Annie and mentioned,

"You might want to go get a nap for a few hours."

"No, I'm fine . . . I promise Toby." Detective Andrew burst in declaring,

"We think we know where Megan is."

"Where?" Toby stood up abruptly, the chair slamming against the wall and repeating, "Where?"

"At Willie's parent's farmhouse . . . in Texas."

"Well how do you figure that?"

"We pulled his record and didn't find anything new but my team contacted the mental institution that Willie was shipped off to when he was little and we discovered his parent's house address."

"How in the hell did this asshole get out?" demanded Mr. Johnson.

"Are you Megan's father?" questioned Mr. Andrews raising his eyebrow in consideration.

"Yes." answered Mr. Johnson walking to the detective.

"Well he turned eighteen and they couldn't keep him any longer because he was legally an adult."

"That's a load of cock-n-bullshit!" yelled Meg's dad angrily.

"Sir, we realize that and if you want to join my team, we'll go find his house and get your daughter back for you."

"Hell yes I'm fucking coming!" He strolled out the front door, following the detectives. Detectives Michael's lingered behind, wanting to offer protection for Annie.

The sun shined brightly through the windows, drowning Megan in sunlight. She flipped to her side, with her back facing Robert. Megan felt two strong hands cup her breasts and press his already hardened manhood against her ass. She peeled her eyes opened murmuring,

"Good morning sunshine."

"Same to you." Robert whispered in her ear,

"I want to go take a shower."

"Well go do it then." His hand snaked around her throat squeezing. Megan grasped his hands, digging her hands in his skin pulling. Robert released Megan and climbed out of bed. She fell back into the pillows gasping for breath.

He said, "If you keep sassing me, I'll let Willie have you and I'll videotape it, mailing your split skull to your father containing the video."

She squirmed out of his grasp and jumped off the bed. Megan stood completely exposed to the one man on the planet that she hoped would never happen. Robert jumped over the mattress, standing before Meagan. He reached down, grabbing her thighs where the screws were still in her flesh. She screamed at Robert while he continued squeezing harder.

"Is that what you want to feel . . . feel this constantly like Chad, Devin, Millie and Clint and Shannon? Huh? I don't have a problem with your body being absorbed in pain. It would actually only turn me on even more."

"Fuck you!" Megan hollered at him, spraying spit mixed with blood at Robert.

"Fuck you too Megan!" He released her thighs saying, "If its pain you want, you'll get your fucking wish." He pushed her back onto the bed and tied her face down onto the red stained sheets. The stench of decay filled Megan's nostrils twisting her gut into knots.

Breathing heavily out of her mouth was the only way to decrease the door. "Lay still bitch, I'll give you pain." Megan's head slammed into the headboard continuously, pain shooting through her head and neck.

"How close are we now?" questioned Mr. Johnson anxiously. He barely remembered what his only daughter looked like.

"We have only a few hours left and I'm sure your daughter is fine." Lied Detective Adams. Mr. Johnson leaned back closing his eyes sliding into a deep uneven sleep.

Chapter Thirty-Three
PUNISHMENT

When Megan woke up, she felt like she had been through hell. She sat up slowly, wincing at the spasms of pain shooting up her spine and legs. The screws were still in her flesh, rotting away. She groaned in pain, tossing the sheet to the floor. Her sticky, blood stained feet touched the hardwood floor, sticking occasionally.

Footsteps stopped in front of her door warning Megan to bury her body beneath the covers with her head deep within the covers muffled the sound of footsteps, walking her way. The mattress flinched under the pressure of someone heavily sitting down. Long, slinky fingers pulled the sheet back, revealing her body. Willie's face beamed at Megan pleased and satisfied. His gaze drifted towards her breasts, a sparkle of desire shining down brightly at them.

He smiled saying, "Do you know how long it's been since I've been a woman?"

"No and frankly I really don't give a rat's ass whether it's been years or your entire fucking murdering career." Megan pulled the sheet up around her chest continuing, "What do you want now?"

"Nothing really . . . oh by the way your cousin, Millie was sweet and delicious." Willie winked at her, running his tongue over his lips. Megan reeled back in disgust as the image of Millie lying atop her bed, squashed beneath Willie's demented human body outraged and sickened Megan.

"You did what to my cousin?"

He smirked saying calmly, "That's right just before I pushed her body down the stairs I ate some of her flesh and drank her blood and oh don't forget I raped her."

"You fucking pig!"

"Thanks." exclaimed Willie.

"That wasn't a damn compliment."

"Hmm . . . do you want to play a game?"

"No."

"Ahh come on Megan, why not?"

"Because I hate you, I hate Robert and did I mention that I hate your stupid, twisted games." shouted Megan.

"Too bad, so sad . . . here Megan put these clothes on and we will have some fun."

"Kiss my ass!" Willie remained sitting on the bed, staring evilly at Megan. "Um . . . hello can I have some privacy?"

"Hell no so get dressed because time is slipping away." She glared hatefully back at Willie, finally deciding to just get it over with. She let the sheet fall to a puddle at her feet while she pulled the t-shirt and shorts on, cringing under the pain.

Robert walked in looking Megan's body over saying,

"It's time for another hide n seek game. Only rule is you have to hide within the house. If Willie catches you, you go with him to his work room but if I catch you then you go with me."

"Don't you think raping somebody can get old?"

"No, honey it's only the beginning." He smiled humorously at her, laughing in his throat.

"Go hide."

Robert and Willie walked into the bathroom, waiting on Megan. She ran down the stairs looking for the first unlocked door. The old grandfather clock in the corner ticked away counting down Megan's last few hours of life. Her hand grasped a door as her feet carried her body down the hallway. As she pushed the door opened slowly, creaks from overhead stopped Megan. She gazed down into the darkness surrounding the stairs dragging her body down into the heavy, blackness.

Concrete slipped beneath her feet at the bottom of the stairs, the wood leaving her. A small light behind a door traveled to Megan, calling safety. She ran into the room, a sea of books corralling her from every corner. Megan backed into a corner, bumping into something warm. Long arms bound themselves around Megan, pressing her arms at her sides. Heavy breathing erupted, quickening Megan's heart.

"Hey Robert I found her!" Robert appeared at the threshold. He leaned against the door frame, crossing his burly arms over his chest, muscles performing their act of intimidation.

He whispered gloomily, "It's time to pay."

"Pay what?"

"Don't be coy with me honey, you know exactly what happens now." Willie flipped Megan's light body over his shoulder taking her to his work room in the barn. She closed her eyes, praying that somebody would show up and save her before it was too late.

Rays from the setting sun, poured down on the black van passing cars left and right.

"Are we almost there?" questioned Megan's father tiredly.

"Yes, sir only one or two hours left."

"What if my daughter isn't there when we show up?"

"Then we keep looking." Mr. Johnson fell against the wall heavily, pulling his phone out, gazing at the time. He ran his hand through his coal, grayish-black hair, hoping they would find Megan, his little girl.

A silver medical table held Megan's body as chains raddled slowly, lowering it to Willie and Robert's level. Hammers, different size knives, a drill, and plates of spikes lay on the small wooden table before Megan, freezing her heart. He pushed Megan's hair out of her face pulling the thick, blonde curly mess into a ponytail holder. Hearing the sound of a liquid being drained into a glass, alarmed Megan. Willie hovered over her back pouring a cold substance on her back watching it devour her blood stained back.

His eyes traveled along the curve of her spine, finally giving into his one and only desire, his hunger and thirst for human blood. He bent forward jutting his tongue out letting it slide gracefully over the surface of the blood. His eyes closed immediately as the cold liquid embraced his taste bud, alerting his demon buried within to consume more. Megan lay there, feeling the way Willie's tongue slid wet and sticky over her spine. She gulped back her tears, trying her damn hardest not to give up to the bastards.

"Just to let you know that your blood sweetens as it gets colder. Imagine that well it's time to get to work." Willie loomed over Megan, holding the drill again, smiling gleefully. Meg gripped the edges of the metal table as she experienced the terrifying feeling of more screws being drilled slowly into her flesh.

She disappeared into a black darkness, losing control of her body, slipping away in and out of consciousness. Willie worked around Megan's body quickly while Robert concentrated on catching Meg's blood as it drained and oozed thinly. Amazed by Willie's work, Robert appraised Willie for his success, knowing exactly what their last act was going to be. The screws heads gleamed out against Megan's legs, drilled accurately into the sides of her legs.

Willie smiled, thrilled with his newest project. The holes in Megan feet, streamed blood loosely while her ribcage proudly presented his came carved deeply into her skin.

"What kind of reward do you want?"

"All I ask Robert is let me keep Megan's blood and the bits of flesh that I nicked and sliced from her body."

"Oh no problem, you can keep all of that, okay?"

"Oh the pleasure was all mine. You know what after she wakes up, I think for supper I will feed her bits and pieces of her own body without her even knowing it."

"Nice." Robert mocked disgustedly.

Voices, rough and deep woke Megan as her vision and hearing blurred in and out.

"You're going to stay here until I say you can leave this damn room." Robert and Willie disposed of Megan's body on the bed, face down with her ankles and wrists tied securely to each bed posts.

She murmured, "What happened to me?"

"How are ya feeling Maggie?" asked Robert ignoring Megan's question.

"Pain . . ."

"Good that is what I wanted you to feel." Robert sat on the edge of the mattress, running his hands through her hair untangling his fingers free, only pushed him to pursue her other body parts that remained neglected during Willie's act earlier. He slid his hands further beneath the covers arousing his manhood.

He sighed saying, "You are all mine because nobody knows where we are except Willie."

"Bastards." mumbled Megan.

"Watch your damn mouth Maggie or I will let Willie sew your lips shut for good."

"Have a nice nap!" shouted Willie.

A wrench dangled before Megan's eyes spreading outward in disbelief and horror. Willie swung the wrench letting it hit Megan's skull with a loud crashing echo. Megan felt a sharp pain radiating through her head, pain wringing throughout her body making her vision focus in and out. The dark, blackness snatched Megan, seducing her back into a world of hideous imaginings.

Chapter Thirty-Four
ONE LAST KISS

A sudden tug of pain erupted throughout Megan's entire body. She lay there not knowing the time, the day, hell she could barely remember who she was. Megan got up and walked unsteadily to the door, surprised to find it unlocked.

She stepped out into the hallway and crossed the oak floor to the bathroom. Megan stared at her reflection in the mirror not believing who the figure was standing before her. Megan splashed cold water on her face, watching it turn from solid clear to muddy red only urged Megan to scream. She closed her eyes, waving her hands in the air frantically.

"Shut the fuck up Maggie!" Her gaze locked on Robert to find him standing there, leaning against the wall, watching her. Megan dropped to the floor, pulling the blood stained sheet around her body tighter. He grinned at his captive, towering over her body saying, "Maggie, you are trapped and you have nowhere to go, my darlin'. You need a shower, I need a shower . . . you are thinking what I'm thinking?"

"How, about I get the fuck out of here?" Megan asked hatefully.

"Don't get smart with me." Robert leaned forward kissing her on the forehead, letting his lips travel downward to find Megan's mouth. "Strip." Robert murmured against her lips.

Robert slammed the door shut, taking no time at all to strip his unwanted jeans off. He repeated urgently,

"Strip." Her whole body shook with rage and defeat. She let the blood soaked sheet fall to the floor in a sea of red as she stood up. Robert's phone rang as he turned the shower on, pushing Megan's body under the water.

He glanced to the ceiling muttering, "I'm going to personality kill him one of these days." Robert's gaze flipped to Megan saying, "Robert here."

"What do you and that little bitch want to eat for supper?"

"I'll fix my own supper, but for you Willie what I want you to do, is fix your famous stew for Megan . . . oh and by the way fuck off." Robert tossed his phone to the counter, climbing into the shower, joining Megan. "Turn around and let me do what I've always wanted to do with you in the shower."

"But . . ." answered Megan as she shrank away from his touch.

"Don't worry I will take care of you." He pushed her body roughly against the tiled wall. Megan squeezed her eyes shut, as the water cascaded down her body, ignoring Robert's hands as they traveled all over her skin.

"Hey, Robert supper's done." Willie hollered as he knocked on the bathroom door, hearing Robert's voice and running water being turned off.

"Okay. Megan and I will be down in a few minutes."

"Okay." Willie left, leaving Robert alone with Megan knowing that he was taking what was rightfully his.

Robert pulled his jeans back on after drying himself off, throwing the towel at Megan's feet, making her pick it up.

"Put this on." ordered Robert. She ignored her body's screams of protest and did as she was told.

"Let's go." Robert pushed Megan to the door continuing, "After we eat, we're getting back down to business."

Willie stood at the stove, drinking a beer, waiting as Robert and Megan walked in the kitchen. A loud knock at the front door silenced them all. Hope drilled through Megan's heart, hope that maybe somebody was here for her.

"Who the fuck is it?" questioned Willie curiously.

"Go see who the fuck it is Willie. I've got Megan." Robert grabbed the handgun off the table saying, "Go get the damn door!"

"It's the fucking cops Robert!" Willie shouted, running back into the kitchen. He grabbed Megan by her hair shouting in her face, "Bitch! Did you have something to do with the damn cops showing up here?"

Willie slapped her across the cheek repeating, "Answer me bitch!"

"Fuck you!"

A loud crashed echoed throughout the house as the front door crashed to the hardwood floor. Robert grabbed Megan by the waist, pinning her arms at her sides while pointing the gun directly at Detective Andrews head, as he yelled with deep control.

"Robert! Let Megan go!" He shook his head no. Hate swarming his soul, not wanting them to take his Maggie away from him again.

Megan whimpered saying, "Robert . . . please don't shoot me." He backed up, stopping as the barrel of a gun pressed against his head.

A voice demanded, "Robert? Let Megan go . . . don't do anything stupid that you will regret."

"Well that's a little too late for that, isn't it?" Willie pointed a 30.6 rifle at an officer standing behind Robert.

"Let her go." Detective Andrews said firmly. He stared at Megan, allowing his eyes to scan the victim before him. Detective Andrews noticed the layers of different shades of bruises. Blood trickled down her legs, farming a small pool at the base of her feet.

"No." said Robert.

As Robert placed his finger on the trigger, Detective Andrews called for backup.

"You want her, come and get her." Three more officers filed in, blocking the exit through the living room.

"Come on Robert and let Megan go. They've caught us fair and square."

"No."

"Think about it before you shoot her or anybody else for that matter." Willie dropped the gun, kicking it at the Detective commenting, "What's it going to be?" Willie reached inside the fridge for a beer, smiling at everyone.

"This." Robert kissed Megan on the lips, pulling the trigger. A shot rang out, hitting Detective Andrews square in the chest. He fell back yelling, as a younger officer shot Robert in the shoulder. Blood squirted out, blasting all over Megan. She gripped her eyes shut falling to the floor with Robert.

She screamed as the blood shot out onto her face. Megan lay, drenched in blood underneath Robert's body. Air slowly drifted downward into her lungs as she tried to regain normal breathing patterns. Detective Andrews helped Megan up, draping a jacket over Megan's body. She sat on the floor, curled up against the counters, clutching the jacket in her fists, drawing it tightly around her body.

He helped her up off the floor, leading Megan outside into the dark, vacant night. A voice Megan barely recognized yelled at her.

"Megan!" She stopped, frozen to the spot standing before her father.

"Daddy?" Megan fainted, dropping to the ground in a heap at her father's feet. Her body slipping into a world of darkness but for once filled with serenity.

"Megan? Megan, listen to me!" shouted her father. "Get an ambulance over here." Two paramedics ran over pulling a stretcher with Detective Haney helping lift Megan off the ground onto the stretcher. As the back doors slammed shut and the lights flipped on, the ambulance sped away with lights and sirens wailing in the distance.

Chapter Thirty-Five
THE END IS NEAR

Megan joined Devin on the hood of his truck, staring at the sparkling stars with him. His fingers intertwined with Megan's, kissing Megan on the forehead saying softly,

"I love you Megan and no matter what happens in the end, I will love you."

"I love you Devin."

Her thoughts raced back to the very first time she ever laid eyes on him, on Robert. Abby's face shined next to her brother's waving at her. Megan smiled and opened her eyes knowing that finally she could rest at peace. After tomorrow she would be free, her soul slowly working its' way back to recovery.

"Tomorrow is the last day of the trial . . . the day you know for damn certain that Robert will never be able to lay eyes or his evil, dirty hands on you ever again."

"I know and I'm ready for tomorrow to come and go forever."

"Well I will be there next to you, holding your hand when they declare his sentence."

"I don't want to talk about it anymore." mumbled Megan. She curled up next to Devin, closing her eyes and drifting off to sleep. Devin pulled her weak body in his arms, carefully placing her body in the cab of his pickup truck. He brought the truck to life, driving off into the dark for his uncle's cabin. Devin turned kissing her on the forehead, saying,

"I love you until the day we die."

EPILOGUE

Megan sat entranced in disbelief that Robert her rapist, her stalker, and murderer was actually going to prison on the accounts for first degree murder, for life without ever attaining parole.

"Robert Anderson, the jury and I have reached a verdict, that we sentence you to the death sentence. You will remain incarcerated in the maximum penitentiary until we have deliberated on the date of your execution."

Her eyes locked with Roberts as he stood, glaring at her. He blew a kiss at her as the Bailiff hand-cuffed Robert leading him out of the courtroom. Megan murmured to her family,

"Did I just hear them say guilty on all charges and will be executed?"

"Yes, honey you won."

Devin pulled Megan into her arms, pressing her body against his. The ring on her wedding finger danced and glistened in the light. She cried softly, pressing her wet, drenched cheeks against Devin's shirt, the silver of scars apparent as her shirt raised a few inches.

"So where do you want to go on vacation for three or four months while your prosecution attorney gets the case for Willie built up and arranged?"

"How, about your aunt's cottage in South Caroline by the beach?"

"Sounds great to me and just to let you know I'm so proud of you baby."

"Thanks for supporting me and never leaving me for one second." He gazed in her eyes, kissing her softly on the lips. She said to Devin and only to Devin,

"Robert deserved what he got, he got his death sentence."